TRIGGER MORTIS

Books by Frank Kane

TRIGGER MORTIS

THE LIVING END

KEY WITNESS

JOHNNY LIDDELL'S MORGUE

A REAL GONE GUY

RED HOT ICE

GRAVE DANGER

POISONS UNKNOWN

BARE TRAP

BULLET PROOF

DEAD WEIGHT

SLAY RIDE

GREEN LIGHT FOR DEATH

ABOUT FACE

by Frank Kane

TRIGGER MORTIS

WILDSIDE PRESS

TRIGGER MORTIS

CHAPTER 1

She was stacked.

Johnny Liddell lounged in the deck chair at the side of the pool, enjoyed the effect as she came toward him. Her copper-colored hair, piled high on her head, glinted metallically in the sunlight. Her body was a warm, nutlike color that few redheads ever achieve. Her mouth was bright in the cocoa color of her face.

As she walked, full breasts swayed rhythmically, threatened to negate the restraint of the thin wisp of brassiere that did a halfhearted job of containing the cantilever construction of her façade. A matching V of bikini was perched perilously high on her hips.

The over-all effect was the impression that her assets were as sound as those of the First National Bank—and as liquid.

She walked over to where Johnny Liddell sat grinning appreciatively. When she smiled, dimples carved white trenches in the tan of her cheeks. Her eyes were green, slightly slanted and crinkled with the smile.

"Sorry to keep you waiting, Johnny." Her voice was low, sultry. "Thanks for coming."

"I wouldn't have missed it for the world."

"Missed what?"

"The entrance. From your last picture?"

Celeste Pierce was this year's Marilyn Monroe and Jayne Mansfield rolled into one. Last year a relative unknown, this year she was a sensation. The movie magazine that had failed to run a bust shot of her on its cover during the past six months was as rare as a war novel without four letter words. Her measurements were more familiar to the average American male than his own license number.

She tossed a manila envelope on the white metal table, dropped into a deck chair facing the private detective. "I guess it's habit. The entrance, I mean." She watched while Liddell lighted two cigarettes, passed one to her. "I didn't ask you to come all the way out to Long Island just to flip a hip at you. I'm in trouble, Johnny. Big trouble. I need your help."

"Who do you want killed?"

The redhead let the smoke dribble from between half-parted lips. "Don't tempt me. I might take you up on it."

"That bad?"

Celeste nodded. "I'm going to be blackmailed."

"Anyone I know?"

The redhead shrugged. "I don't know myself who's behind it. They just sent me a sample of what they have to show me what I'm up against."

"The softener, eh? Convincing?"

"Very convincing." The girl looked down at her highly shellacked nails, long lashes half veiling her eyes. "Nothing you could argue with."

"Pictures?"

Celeste nodded. She reached over for the envelope, dropped it into his lap. "Pictures and an article already set in type. It's called 'When Celeste Pierce was Sarah Peters—She Was the Specialty of the House.' The pictures back it up."

Liddell scowled at the envelope, tossed it back on the table.

"You're not going to help me?"

"Of course I'll help you. I'll take your word for what's in the envelope."

"Thanks." The redhead took a last deep drag on the butt, dropped it to the concrete rim of the pool, crushed it out. "I'm not yelling frame, Johnny. They're pictures of me and I'm not very proud of them. I'm willing to buy them back."

"Where do I come in?"

"I need your help to make sure that all sales are final."

Liddell scowled at the blue-green water of the pool, the reflection of the white furniture that lined it. "They haven't set the time or place for the pay-off?"

"No. A note with that stuff just said they'd contact me after I had a chance to think it over."

"When did you get the stuff?"

"Yesterday afternoon. I didn't know what to do. Not that I had any choice, but I wanted to make sure that whatever I did do was the right thing. That's why I called you."

"I don't know if you did the right thing calling me." He brought his eyes back from the water to her face.

"You said you'd help me."

"I'm not much of a guy at handling pay-offs, baby. My first impulse is to take shakedown artists apart like a fifty-cent watch."

The redhead caught her full lower lip between her teeth and worried it. "For my sake don't."

"Can't somebody from the studio handle it for you?"

"I'm afraid to ask." She laid her hand on his thigh. "I'm just beginning to make it out there, Johnny. But if something like this breaks I'm afraid they'll back away from me like I had the plague."

"I see what you mean. Okay, I'll handle it for you. Do you know what the tab is going to be?"

6

"No."

Liddell grunted. "How high can I go?"

"I can raise ten thousand if I have to."

"Ten thousand? They must be some pictures! You could buy an old master for that."

The redhead grinned ruefully. "I wasn't exactly an amateur myself."

"Who'd be likely to know about the pictures and the fact that Celeste Pierce was Sarah Peters?"

The redhead chewed at her lip, scowled in concentration. "Not too many people. Vinny D'Amato would. He was the booker."

"Stags?"

The girl nodded, dropped her eyes to her lap. "He probably took the pictures. He was always fooling around cameras and stuff"—she looked up—"but wouldn't I have seen the flash?"

"Not if he used infrared. Who else?"

She shook her head, scowled. After a moment, her brow cleared. She snapped her fingers. "Les Ringer."

Liddell pulled out an envelope, scribbled the name on the back. "Who's he?"

"A Poverty Row press agent. He'd manage to crack a few lines into Walker or Winchell every so often. He worked for D'Amato." She made a moue. "A slimy little creep. He used to get accounts by digging up girls for people who could do him some good. Used to use the line that the guy he was pimping for could get them screen tests. The kids used to go for it big."

"You?"

The redhead shook her head. "I just told you I wasn't an amateur. When the chance came to get a screen test I didn't need any Les Ringer to set it up for me."

"Where can I find this character?"

"I don't know. But he usually came out of the woodwork about seven at night and made the rounds. I used to bump into him regularly at Ransom's Drugstore on 46th." Her eyes searched Liddell's face. "What are you going to do?"

"Find out who has those pictures. Maybe we can get them back before they can put the squeeze on."

"But if it goes wrong?"

"Then you'll get up the money. You don't lose a thing."

"You think Ringer has them?"

Liddell shrugged. "You said there was an article as well as pictures. Right?"

The girl nodded.

"As I remember D'Amato, he had enough trouble spelling his name without trying to write articles." He flipped the cigarette into the grass. "A press agent, now that's another thing. He might be able to lay enough words next to each other to make an article."

"But suppose there are copies. Suppose he tries to——"

Liddell grinned. "It's been tried. I think we can persuade Ringer to part with the negatives and all. Or tell us where we can get them."

"You're sure this is the right way to handle it, Johnny? I can't afford for anything to go wrong."

"Nothing will go wrong, baby. I'll treat him as carefully as an atom bomb." He checked his watch. "You say he usually makes his rounds after seven?"

The redhead nodded. "He used to. I guess he still does."

"It'll take me almost an hour to get back into town. I'd better start back now. Maybe we can wrap this thing up tonight."

"If you get them back, will you let me know as soon as you can?"

Liddell grinned at her. "I'll do better than that. I'll bring them out myself. It might be late."

"It wouldn't be too late."

CHAPTER 2

Ransom's Drugstore
is the headquarters for young hopefuls and tiring
oldsters of the theatrical district. Any evening its
stools might be occupied by chorines, columnists,
refugees from Hollywood or members of the fringe
of the fight mob that used to congregate along Jacobs' Beach.

The East Coast counterpart of Hollywood's
Schwab's, the infrequent tourist who might stumble
into the store would be amazed to see a reigning film
favorite or the star of a hit show on 45th Street waiting on themselves behind the counter. Rubbing el-
bows with a racketeer who is waiting out the verdict
on a deportation trial might be the star of last night's
television spectacular.

Johnny Liddell walked in, found a stool near
the end of the counter, slid onto it. He told the wavy-

haired counterman whose lips and cheeks were suspiciously rosy that he wanted a coffee and Danish. While the man behind the counter was sloshing a thick black liquid from a Silex into a cup, Liddell looked around. The place was just beginning to fill up and some of the regulars had taken possession of their usual stools for the evening.

"Will that be all?" The counterman's voice was a little on the shrill side. He cocked an impatient eyebrow at Liddell, waited with his pencil poised over the check.

"Les Ringer in yet tonight?"

"It doesn't look that way." He pointed daintily toward a bank of telephone booths in the rear. "His office is empty."

"His office?" Liddell frowned down at the booths.

"The second booth from the end. The way he takes it over they should make him pay rent." He tapped the check with the pencil. "Will that be all?"

Liddell nodded, watched him scribble a total on the bill, mince toward the other end of the counter where he welcomed a blondined chorus boy effusively.

Liddell was on his third cigarette when a heavy-set man in a loud plaid sports jacket and charcoal slacks walked in. A stained grey fedora sat on the back of his head, a toothpick protruded from the corner of his thick lips. He headed for the second booth from the end.

As the heavy-set man settled himself in the booth, Liddell slid off the stool, walked casually toward the phones. The man inside the booth was stuffing a dime into the slot, dialing with a pudgy forefinger.

"Any calls for me, Myrt?" he yelled across the room to the counterman.

The wavy-haired man dropped the hand of the chorus boy, flashed a venomous glance at the booth. "Why should I take your calls? And don't call me Myrt."

The man in the booth chuckled, pressed his lips toward the mouthpiece. "Hello. Is Danton around? This is Les Ringer." He nodded disgustedly. "You don't know where he's going to be any time tonight, do you? I thought I might bump into him, and—" he broke off, listened for a minute—"well, it's a pretty hot item and I wanted to give it to him before I pass it along to the other boys. Yeah. Sure. If you do, tell him I'll try to make a meet with him someplace tonight."

He hung up the phone, mumbled under his breath, shoveled another dime into the slot. He was dialing the number of the *Daily Mirror* when Liddell's bulk blocked off some of the light.

Ringer scowled up at him. "Sorry, pal. This booth'll be busy for a long time. Find yourself another Ameche." He went back to his dialing, frowned his annoyance to find Liddell still cutting off the light. "Now, look, friend——"

Liddell reached in, jiggled the hook, waited until the dime had been returned. "I wouldn't want it to cost you any money. You and I have some talking to do."

Some of the belligerence had drained from Ringer's face. "You'll have to catch me sometime when I'm not busy," he blustered. "I don't just—" he stared at Liddell for a moment—"Hey, I make you. You're a dick, ain't you?"

"We can't talk here. Let's go to your place."

Ringer licked at his lips. "I told you I'm busy. I——"

Liddell caught him by the lapel, pulled him to his feet. "We're going to your place. How you go is up to you. You can walk or I can put you on wheels and roll you."

"You can't get away with pushing me around, mister. You try and——"

Liddell jabbed his fingers into the heavy man's midsection right under the ribs. Ringer's breath whooshed out of him, he collapsed to the seat gasping for his breath. Liddell reached down, caught him

13

under the arm, pulled him to his feet. Ringer didn't resist, stared at him, the whites of his eyes showing under the colorless discs of his pupils.

"Where's your pad?"

Ringer licked at his lips, his eyes darted from side to side, came to rest on Liddell's face. "The Hotel William. Around the corner."

"Look, Ringer. You behave and we have a little talk. You play games and you have big trouble." He flicked back his lapel, let the wide eyes see the .45 nestled in the shoulder holster. "We're going to walk out of here to your place. Give me a hard time and you're in a good spot to find out if you can outrun a slug."

Perspiration gleamed on the heavy man's upper lip and along his hairline. "This is crazy. You can't—" he broke off, nodded—"okay. I got nothing to hide." His eyes tried to meet Liddell's, couldn't.

Liddell stepped aside, let Ringer sidle by him. The press agent shuffled toward the door, Liddell a pace behind him, slightly to his right.

"You leaving early?" the man behind the counter taunted. "What happened? Did you finally place that item and put yourself out of business?" The chorus boy giggled his appreciation, Ringer looked neither right nor left, led the way through the revolving door.

Broadway was already filling up with the slow

moving crowd that seems to ebb and flow from 42nd Street to 52nd and back every hour of the night from six, when the officeworkers meet their dates in front of the Paramount, until four the next morning when the Latin Quarter spills its last patrons into 48th Street and traffic dwindles to almost nothing.

Ringer swung off Broadway onto 46th Street, led the way to a dingy stone building that was identified by an electric blinker as the "Hotel William." Tonight, some bulbs were burned out so it read simply "Hot. . Will. . ."

It was an old weather-beaten stone building hemmed in by similarly weatherbeaten buildings that line the south side of streets between Broadway and Sixth Avenue. A threadbare and faded carpet ran the length of a lobby that had long since given up any pretense of serving a useful purpose. The chairs were rickety and unsafe, the rubber plants grimed with dust.

An old man behind the registration desk raised watery eyes as they entered, then dropped them back to a perusal of the scratch sheet spread out on the desk. A pimpled youth with slack mouth and discolored sacs under his eyes stood alongside an empty elevator cage, watched them dully as they approached.

"Back early tonight, huh, Les?" He waited until

15

Liddell had followed the heavy man into the cage, slammed the metal door.

Ringer, his eyes fixed on the bulge under Liddell's arm, merely grunted. At the fourth floor, the doors slammed open, he led the way down the corridor to a door in the rear. He stopped in front of 408, looked at Liddell, got no encouragement, dipped his hand into his pocket, brought out a key.

The room beyond had a lone window that faced on an air shaft with the blank stone wall of the building adjoining less than six feet away. An unmade bed revealed grey linen, clothing was strewn over the back of the only chair in the room. A bridge lamp spilled a sickly yellow light into the room, exposed the backing of the carpet where the nap had been worn away in front of the chair. The only other door in the room opened into a small lavatory.

Liddell kicked the door shut behind him. "Cozy little place you have here."

"So it's a dump," Ringer snarled. "You come here to write the place up for *House Beautiful?*"

"That's not my racket, writing for magazines. I thought it was yours."

The heavy man stared at him. "What's that supposed to mean?" Bubbles formed and broke in the center of his lips. "I'm a press agent, not a hack."

"Ever hear of an article called 'When Celeste

16

Pierce was Sarah Peters'? I thought you wrote that one."

Ringer wiped the wet smear of his mouth with the back of his hand. "You're making with the mouth, friend, but you're not getting to me. You're not making sense."

Liddell walked over to the man, caught him by the front of his jacket, pushed him back into the chair. "Look, buster. I've got a client named Celeste Pierce. You have something that belongs to her. Pictures. I came to pick them up."

Ringer shook his head stubbornly, stared down at his hands in his lap. "I don't dig it, mister. You got the wrong Joe."

Liddell caught a hand full of the heavy man's hair, pulled his head back. "I told you it could mean big trouble if you gave me a hard time. You got those pictures from D'Amato. You wrote an article to go with them. You want to sell, maybe we're in the market to buy. But make me find them myself and you get nothing—except maybe a hole in the head. That get to you?"

The man in the chair stared up into Liddell's face, the perspiration beading on his forehead. "I got nothing to sell, mister. Honest."

Liddell yanked the head back farther, water came to the heavy man's eyes. "You never saw the pictures?"

"All right, all right. So D'Amato did give me the pictures and I did do the article. But I haven't got them"—he winced as Liddell tightened his hold—"I sold them."

"Who to?"

The coarse tongue licked at his lips again. *Bare Facts* magazine. They buy a lot of that stuff."

Liddell let go the hair, wiped the oil from his fingers on the other man's coat. "And you provide a lot of it?"

Ringer shrugged. "So I get to know a lot about some of these characters. There's nothing wrong with peddling what I know."

"You pimp for them and then finger them for a scandal rag. No, nothing wrong," he sneered. "Not a thing."

"Who are you to make cracks? Just a lousy shamus who——"

Liddell lashed out, caught Ringer across the mouth with the back of his hand, knocked his head to one side. The bubbles that formed and broke in the center of the heavy man's mouth were pink tinged now.

"Who did you deal with at *Bare Facts?*"

Ringer put the side of his hand to his mouth, stared with stricken eyes at the pink stain it brought away. "The big boss. Murray Carter." He cringed back when he thought Liddell might hit him again.

"I'll have a little talk with Carter. But if I were you, I wouldn't break the news to him that I'm coming. Because then I might have to come back and have another talk with you. Only longer."

When he walked out of the room, the heavy man was dabbing at his battered lips with a wadded, grey-colored handkerchief.

CHAPTER 3

The telephone on the night table started to shrill discordantly. Johnny Liddell groaned, cursed sleepily and dug his head further into the pillow. The noise refused to go away.

He opened one eye experimentally; he could see by the half-drawn shade that it was still night. He glowered at the phone, but it refused to be impressed and continued to shrill at him.

He tried to wipe the sleep from his eyes but it wouldn't wipe. The phone gave no indication of giving up, so he fumbled for it, located it and held it to his ear.

"Yeah?"

"Johnny? I've been trying to reach you all evening." It was Celeste Pierce's voice, but some of the sultry quality had gone from it. There was a note of hysteria in it. "I've got to see you right away."

Liddell peered at the clock on the night table and groaned. "You got any idea what time it is? It's after three."

"I tried to reach you, but——"

"I know. My answering service picked up the calls and I called you back, but——"

"I've got to see you, Johnny. Please."

"Where are you?"

"In an all-night drugstore on Forty-ninth Street."

Liddell raked his fingers through his hair, nodded. "Okay. Grab a cab. Know where I am?"

"No. Your service gave me your number but they wouldn't give me your address."

"Carson Apartments on Forty-eighth east of Park. Apartment 2 B."

"I'll be right there."

Liddell dropped the receiver back on its hook, swore softly. He swung his feet from under the covers to the cold floor, then completed the waking-up process in the bathroom by dousing his face with cold water. He was just finished running a comb through his hair when the phone rang. It was the towheaded night clerk on the desk.

"You expecting anyone, Johnny?"

Liddell grunted. "Yeah. Send her up."

"She's already on the way. I figured a chick like this if you don't want, we won't have any trouble disposing of." He made no attempt to hide the envy in his voice. "No wonder you keep such lousy office hours."

"It's not that. We got a lousy union." There was a knock on the door, he dropped the receiver back on its hook. "Coming."

When he opened the door, he was shocked by the change in the girl's appearance. The cocoa-colored skin had a yellowish tinge, the green eyes were wide with shock. The full lower lip had developed a twitch which she had difficulty in controlling.

She darted in, leaned against the wall while he closed the door behind her.

"What's with you?" Liddell wanted to know.

The redhead's face contorted, she started to cry. "I killed him, Johnny. They'll be after me. I killed him."

Liddell started to answer, thought better of it, led her to a chair and pushed her into it. "You need a drink." He headed for the kitchen, reappeared with two glasses half filled with ice. "What'll it be?"

The girl had lighted a cigarette, was smoking with short, nervous puffs. She seemed to have regained control. "VO if you have it."

Liddell walked over to a cabinet, opened the door. He brought out a fifth of VO and a half-filled fifth of Ancient Age. He spilled a stiff hooker of the Canadian over the ice, handed it to the girl.

"Get this inside you. Then we'll talk."

He waited while the girl took a deep swallow of the whiskey, coughed, leaned her head back against the chair. After a moment, she opened her eyes. "I shouldn't have come here. There's no reason for you to get mixed up in it."

"Mixed up in what?"

"I just told you. I killed him."

"You killed who?"

"The man who was trying to blackmail me."

"Murray Carter?"

The redhead's jaw dropped, her eyes widened. "How do you know?"

Liddell sighed, added more VO to the girl's glass. "Les Ringer told me he sold the article and the pictures to *Bare Facts*. I was going to see Carter in the morning." He poured himself a fast drink, tossed it off. "What happened?"

"He called me tonight. Said he had this article and was going to publish it. But that maybe we could talk it over. I tried to reach you, but your answering service didn't know where you were. Finally, I decided I'd go by myself."

Liddell swore softly. "If only you had stalled him."

"I tried to, but he wouldn't let me. He said he had to decide tonight whether or not the article was going to run. Tomorrow would be too late. From the way he talked, I got the idea I might be able to make a deal."

"What time was this?"

She caught her lower lip between her teeth. "He called about nine. Wanted me up there by midnight."

"Anyone see you going in?"

"I don't think so." She sipped at her drink, studied Liddell over the rim. "There's a night clerk on duty, but I don't think he saw me. He has sort of a little office off the desk, and—" she broke off, looked stricken—"the elevator boy. He's sure to remember my going up there."

"It figures. Anybody in Carter's place when you went in?"

The redhead shook her head. "He was alone, working at a desk." She set her glass down, rubbed the backs of her arms as though she were cold. "At first he was fairly nice. He poured me a drink and we talked about people we both knew in Hollywood or around town, just as if it was a social visit. Then, after about an hour, he got down to business."

Liddell nodded for her to continue.

"He pulled out this article and the pictures and made a big production of looking them over. I figured this was it, sort of a casting-couch deal in reverse. I waited for the pass or the proposition. It was a proposition, all right—but not the kind I expected."

"What kind of a proposition was it?"

"He wanted me to bird-dog material for his magazine. Get stories about people in Hollywood, put the finger on queers. Stuff like that." She drained her glass, set it down. "If I'd do that, he'd give me my article and the pictures back. If I didn't, he said it would be the lead story in the next issue of *Bare Facts*."

Liddell scratched the side of his nose with his index finger. "You told him no."

The redhead stared at him for a minute. "Look, Johnny, I told you I wasn't proud of how I made a living before I got a break. But I was a hungry kid then. I'm not hungry enough now to work that kind of a filthy racket. I'd rather go back to being the specialty of the house."

"So you spit in his eye. What then?"

"He sort of went crazy. Called me all kinds of names, kept shoving the pictures under my nose, stuff like that. That I could take, but when he started slapping me around, that I couldn't take."

"And I had to be wasting my time with that fat louse of a Ringer." He added some Ancient Age to his glass. "Go on."

"There was a gun on the desk he had been sitting at. I grabbed the gun"—she broke off, the color drained from her face, leaving the make-up as garish smears in the yellowness of her complexion—"he came at me like a crazy man and I started squeezing the trigger. I kept squeezing it until the gun was empty."

"You're sure he's dead?"

The redhead nodded. "He's dead all right. The blood spurted from his mouth, he fell back into a chair." She plucked at her lip with a shaking hand. "It was pretty rugged."

"I know."

"What do I do, Johnny? Give myself up?"

Liddell walked over to the window, pulled back the curtain, stared down into the darkened street. "Better let me take a look around up there first. Maybe he's not dead. Even if he is, we may be able to figure some way to keep you out of it."

"But I killed him."

He swung around from the window. "I stepped on a cockroach this morning. That doesn't mean I should give myself up, does it?" He walked back to where she was sitting. "You didn't think to pick up the pictures and the article?"

She shook her head. "It wouldn't have done any good. It wasn't the originals of the pictures. They're still around some place."

"Maybe I can find them."

She put her hand on his arm. "I have no right to ask you to do that, Johnny. I'm not sorry he's dead. He would have ruined me anyhow; this way I at least had the satisfaction of paying him back."

"Where did Carter live?"

"The Graumont on Fiftieth. The penthouse."

Liddell walked to the closet, brought out a shoulder holster, shrugged into it. He covered it with a jacket. "You'd better stay here until I have a chance to look the situation over. I'll get back as soon as I can."

The towheaded clerk on the desk stared at Liddell with unconcealed wonder as he watched the private detective cross the lobby, wave down a cab.

"With that upstairs, he sure picks a helluva time to go riding," he complained to nobody in particular.

CHAPTER 4

The Graumont
is a huge pile of concrete and plate glass overlooking
the East River at 50th Street. A gaily-colored awning
ran from the entrance to the curb, flapping desul-
torily in the breeze from the river.

Johnny Liddell pushed through the plate-glass
door, ploughed through the deep pile carpeting toward the bank of elevators in the rear. Behind the
desk off to the right, an old man in a dark jacket
dabbed at rheumy eyes with his handkerchief. He
watched Liddell's progress across the lobby with no
show of curiosity.

Inside the elevator, a small placard advised that
"From 2 A.M. to 7 A.M., all elevator service will be
self service." Liddell noted that the penthouse was on
the twentieth floor, pushed the button for the eighteenth floor for the benefit of the rheumy-eyed man
behind the desk.

When the cage whooshed to a sighing stop on the eighteenth floor, Liddell got out, headed down the corridor to where a red light marked the staircase. He climbed two flights and stopped at the penthouse door. He tried the knob, found the door locked. From an inside pocket he brought a thin strip of celluloid, fitted it into the door above the lock. After a moment, he was rewarded by the sound of a faint click. The knob turned easily in his hand, he pushed the door open.

The room beyond was half office, half den. Against the far wall, a highly polished desk faced the big picture window that overlooked the river.

In front of a fireplace a man sat in a big leather chair staring at him with unseeing eyes. A red stream ran from the corner of his mouth, had dripped down to a large matching stain that darkened the front of his white shirt.

Liddell closed the door behind him, transferred the .45 from its holster to his right hand. There were two doors leading into the room, besides the door through which he had entered. Both were closed.

Softly he walked to the door nearest him, pushed it open, fanned it with his gun. Empty.

The door next to it was obviously the bedroom. He turned the knob cautiously, pushed it open, stepped back out of range. After a moment, he reached in, flicked on the light. The bedroom, too, was empty.

He slipped the .45 back into its hammock, walked back to where Murray Carter sat staring tirelessly at the door. On the table beside him were two glasses with half-melted ice cubes and a trace of liquor.

Liddell stuck his fingers into one of the glasses, spread them so he could lift the glass without defacing any possible prints on the outside of it. He breathed on it. The smudges told him that someone had taken the precaution of wiping the glass clean.

He held it to his nose, sniffed. He sniffed again, then held the glass to his lips, tasted the contents. Bourbon. He repeated the process with the other glass. The prints had not been wiped from that glass, were probably those of Carter himself. The glass had contained Scotch.

He looked around the room, located the portable bar next to the fireplace. On it were an assortment of bottles. He examined the labels, found Old Grand-Dad, VO, Haig & Haig Pinch, House of Lords Gin and Four Roses. He replaced the bottles, started back to where the dead man sat, almost stumbled when he saw the damp spot in the back of Carter's head. He walked closer, parted the hair carefully, saw the unmistakable sign of where a bullet had ripped through the back of the man's head.

There was no corresponding hole for the exit of the slug.

Liddell scowled, measured the distance from the back of the chair to the wall.

"Damn funny a slug that would make a hole that size wouldn't go through," he mused, "unless it was deflected by the cranial wall. But why no powder marks?"

He stepped back, sought some indication that the body or the chair had been moved, found none. He walked around to the front of the chair, studied the dead man carefully. Then, taking a fresh handkerchief from his breast pocket, he deliberately dampened it with the clotting blood on the man's chest.

He had barely straightened up when the telephone on the desk started to ring. He debated the advisability of answering it, let it ring four times. On the fifth ring, he picked it up.

"Mr. Carter?" The voice sounded rusty. "This is Nelson on the desk. I got a call for you here. Man was real insistent. I didn't want to wake you, but" —there was a pause—"that's funny. He must of hung up. I hope I didn't disturb you, but he insisted that——"

Liddell held his hands across his lips lightly. "I was asleep, Nelson. I don't want to be disturbed. By nobody until tomorrow afternoon."

"Sure, Mr. Carter. I just didn't want you to think that——"

Liddell cut him off by replacing the receiver on the hook. It seemed like the way Murray Carter would have handled the situation. He walked back to the desk, wrapped the stained handkerchief in another and replaced them in his pocket.

Then he set about searching the desk drawers. There were plenty of exposé articles on the famous, once famous and near famous. He selected half a dozen, stuck them in a manila envelope. No place could he find the article on Celeste Pierce. Finally, he gave it up. After he had satisfied himself that he had left no traces of his presence in the apartment, he turned off the light, carefully closed the door after him.

When he reached the lobby, the rheumy-eyed old man had retired to his little office off the desk.

He picked up a cab at the corner of First and 50th and gave the address of the Carson Apartments to the cabby, whose name card claimed for him the improbable label of Aloysius McAteer. Liddell was still puzzling over what he had found at the Graumont when the cab bounced its front tire off the curb to announce its arrival at its destination.

Aloysius McAteer seemed suitably impressed by the dollar tip, ground the car into gear and roared off on the off-chance that it might have been a mistake.

On the way in, Liddell stopped at the desk.

"She's still up there," the towhead leered.

"You won't forget what time she arrived and what time she leaves, will you?" Liddell asked him.

"Not if you say so." He glanced at the clock. "It was a little before three when she got here. It's now about four-thirty and she's still here." He looked back to Liddell. "Someone likely to ask?"

"It could be." He slid a folded ten across the counter. "And if they do, there'd be no reason to mention that I happened to go out for a little while, would there?"

"You think I'm crazy? What kind of a place would they think we were running if I told anybody that Celeste Pierce comes to visit a guest in his room and he goes out for a ride?"

At the door of his apartment, Liddell rapped softly. "Okay, open up. It's me," he whispered.

The door was opened a crack, an eye appeared at the opening. Then he heard the sound of a chain being removed and the door swung wide open.

The redhead had changed from her clothes into a pair of his pajamas. The sleeves and trouser legs were rolled up, the blouse hung down almost to her thighs and the seat of the trousers bagged ludicrously. She eyed Liddell anxiously.

33

"You've been there?" She closed the door behind him, rebolted it and leaned against it.

Liddell nodded, dropped his hat and the manila envelope on the table. "I've been there."

"He——"

Liddell nodded. "He's still there. In the chair in front of the fireplace." He walked over to the dresser, spilled some Ancient Age into the glasses they had used earlier, handed one to the girl. "He's dead all right."

The redhead raised her glass to her lips, took a swallow. She started to cough, held the glass away from her. "What is it?" she gasped.

"Bourbon."

She shook her head, her eyes watered. "I can't drink bourbon. I'm allergic or something." She wiped her eyes with the back of her hand. "Do you have any Canadian?"

"Sorry." Liddell poured the contents of the girl's glass into his, got her some VO. "You couldn't accidentally drink bourbon and not realize it?"

Celeste shook her head. "This always happens. I'm sorry."

Liddell walked wearily over to the couch, dropped onto it. "Don't be. It proves someone else was in Carter's apartment after you left."

"What proves that?"

"There were two glasses on the table next to

where Carter was sitting. One held Scotch, the other bourbon. Carter was drinking Scotch, wasn't he?"

The redhead nodded.

"Then the last person to be with Carter was a bourbon drinker. He's probably the killer."

"I am. I told you I killed him. I told you how it happened."

"Tell me again."

"Must I?"

"Yeah."

The girl took a deep breath. "I grabbed the gun. He came at me. I emptied the whole revolver into him. He was covered with blood."

"I know. His whole shirt was covered with it."

"So I killed him."

Liddell shook his head. "Not unless you can throw a curve with a .32 slug. Carter was killed by a bullet behind his ear."

"But how could he be? I tell you I shot him in the stomach. Five times right in the stomach. I ought to know. I squeezed the trigger."

"But you didn't kill him. The somebody who was with him later and who drank bourbon. That's who killed him."

Celeste walked over to the window, stared out. "You're trying to cover for me, Johnny. But it won't work. I was seen going up there——"

"At about twelve. The old man probably saw

you leaving. What time would you say that was?"

She continued to stare down into the street. "About three."

"That same clerk is going to be able to testify that Carter was alive at four-thirty—over an hour after you left."

The girl swung around. "How could he?"

"Carter answered a telephone call at four-thirty."

"You?"

Liddell nodded. "The phone kept ringing. I took a chance on answering it. Whoever it was had hung up."

She walked over to where he sat. Even the baggy pajama coat couldn't hide the fluid rhythm of her breasts. "Johnny, you were there a long time. You didn't——"

"Cover for you by firing a slug into the back of his head?" He shook his head. "I didn't have to. It was there when I arrived."

"But he must have been already dead. I couldn't have missed. Not five times that close." She sat close to him on the couch, the warmth of her thighs against his. "And you did give me the alibi."

"Not me. The killer."

"How do you mean?"

"I think he was calling, knowing that Carter was already dead. He kept after the clerk to keep ringing.

He probably figured that when the clerk couldn't raise Carter he'd send someone up and they'd find the body."

"But why?"

Liddell shrugged. "To pinpoint the time. He must have had an alibi all set for that time and he didn't want it to go to waste."

"But what were you doing all that time?"

"Trying to find the article on you and the original pictures. They weren't there. A lot of other stuff." He pointed to the thick manila envelope under his hat. "I picked out the worst of it figuring maybe it would point to the real killer."

Her mouth was an O of amazement. "You mean you took that risk? Calmly searched the place knowing the cops might break in any minute?" She leaned close to him, her breath warm and fragrant on his cheek. "That was really sticking your neck out."

"Well, we've got to work fast if we're going to keep your name out of this. And the best way to do it is to find the real killer. I think we have a couple of hours' leeway. Until tomorrow afternoon maybe."

"But how? Won't they find him when——"

Liddell grinned glumly. "When the clerk talked to him a little while ago, Carter told him he didn't want to be disturbed by anyone for anything until tomorrow afternoon. By then, we may be able to come up with something."

"You sure do go all out for a client, Johnny. I'm really grateful." She looked down at the bulky, shapeless pajamas. "Not that a girl could really look grateful in an outfit like this."

Liddell cocked an eyebrow humorously. "You're a girl?"

She pouted, stood up, raised her hands to her hair and loosened it. It fell in molten cascade over her shoulders. She unbuttoned the coat of the pajamas, slid it back over her shoulders. The uniform cocoa color of her body was striped in dazzling white where the top of her bikini had been. Her breasts were firm, tiptilted. As she loosened the string of her pajamas, Liddell whistled softly.

"You're a girl," he conceded.

CHAPTER 5

The clock
on the table next to the bed showed 9:30. The drawn shades gave the room the dimness of night. The redhead on the bed stirred uneasily, opened heavy-lidded eyes, stared around the unfamiliar room. Suddenly she sprang to wide-eyed wakefulness, sat up and pulled the blanket around her.

"Liddell! Liddell, where are you?"

The door to the bathroom opened, spilled a yellow triangle of light into the room. Liddell walked out, drying his still damp hair.

"Shower wake you, baby? I'm sorry. Go on back to sleep."

"What are you doing up so early?"

Liddell grinned, balled the damp towel and tossed it back into the bathroom. "So early? I've been reading that filth since six o'clock"—he nodded toward the stacked material he had brought from

Carter's apartment—"he sure gave enough people a good reason to punch holes through his head."

"You think you've got a lead from them?"

Liddell considered, shrugged. "Far as I know, most of the ones with the best reason for wanting him dead are out on the Coast."

"Except me."

"We've already excepted you. I told you last night you didn't kill him. If a little hunch I have pans out, I'll be able to prove it. Even to you." He sat on the side of the bed. "I've only seen this character when he was dead. Give me some idea of what he looked like alive." He picked up an envelope and a pencil from the night table. "How tall would you say he was?"

The redhead wrinkled her brow in concentration. "Not too tall. Maybe five seven, weighed maybe one forty. He had a mean mouth—you know, thin lips that looked like he was always sneering. A big nose, but you could see that. Squinty eyes."

Liddell nodded. "He wore his hair in a three-quarter part. Right?" He looked up. "Notice any scars or moles? Looked to me like there might have been one right along here." He ran his index finger along the side of his jaw. "I didn't want to move the body to check it."

The girl considered, bobbed her head. "There

was a scar right there. About three inches long. It got real red when he got mad."

Liddell got up, stuck the envelope in his pocket, grinned at her. "Now we go to work."

"Johnny, are you sure it wouldn't be better for everybody if I just gave myself up and——"

He leaned over, tilted her chin with the tip of his finger, covered her mouth with his. "You'll have to trust me."

"I do."

"Well, unless you pull that blanket up, you're liable to lose faith in your own judgment."

"I wish you didn't have to go, Johnny. I wish you'd stay with me today. I need protection."

"By me or from me?"

The B.C.I., the Bureau of Criminal Identification, at Police Headquarters, is located on the first floor. Johnny Liddell walked in, consulted the huge chart on the wall on which are listed all sixty-two varieties of crime encountered by the department. The crimes are listed alphabetically from arson all the way down to worthless checks. Each crime is further broken down into subdivisions and alongside each is the number of the file in which known operators in that category are listed.

Liddell checked, found that extortionists were listed in Files D and E. These files are in what is known to the public as the rogues' gallery, to the department as the gallery, to the experts as the M.O. file.

Files D and E contained hundreds of records and pictures of men who had been either indicted or convicted of extortion. They were broken down by height.

Liddell pulled out a drawer in the steel filing cabinet devoted to men in the five-seven bracket. After flipping through hundreds of cards, he failed to come up with a make. He tried five-six and five-eight on the chance that the girl had mistaken Carter's height. None of the faces struck him as that of the dead man in the chair and there was no record on a Murray Carter.

He moved over to another file marked "Facial Deformities—White." Under five seven there were about a hundred cards, showing face and profile of known extortionists with particular attention to scars or other facial deformities.

He had flipped through less than a third of the cards in the drawer when he stopped, stared at the face and profile of a thin-faced man with a large nose. It was a picture of a man much younger than the man he had seen in the chair and death had not yet caused the features to sag grotesquely. But the thick hair was combed in a three-quarter part and a three-inch scar ran along the line of the jaw.

The card identified the man as "Murray Cartman, alias Morris Cartman, alias Morris Carter." It listed two convictions for fraud in the early thirties and three *nolle prossed* indictments for extortion. Liddell transferred the information to the back of the envelope containing Carter's description. He softly slid the drawer back into place.

Outside in the corridor, Johnny Liddell headed for the open grillwork elevator, rode a wheezing, jolting cage to the fifth floor where the police laboratory is located.

Lieutenant Eddie Michaelson, chemist in charge, was peering nearsightedly at a bubbling orange solution in the bottom of a test tube when Johnny Liddell walked in. He set the test tube into a rack, wiped his hands on his lab apron.

"Hi, Mike," Liddell greeted him. "Busy?"

The chemist shrugged. "Always busy. Always have plenty of time."

"Time to do me a favor?"

Michaelson grinned. "Depends on the favor." He watched while Liddell brought the wadded handkerchief from his pocket, unrolled it to expose the bloodstained one it covered. "What could your boys tell me about that blood?"

The lieutenant plucked at his long, thin nose with thumb and forefinger. "Well, we can tell you whether it came from a mammal, fish, bird or reptile.

43

If from a mammal, if it's human blood. If from a human, under which of the seventy-two different types it can be classified. That enough?" He picked the handkerchief up, held it under the light. "I guess what you're really interested in is whether it's human or not. Right?"

Liddell nodded. "Would that take long?"

"A couple of hours. I've got to make a saline solution of it for precipitin reaction." He looked up from the handkerchief. "You got any reason to doubt it's human?"

Liddell shrugged. "It came off the shirt of an old-time con man. I've got a sneaking hunch it was a cackle-bladder cool-off."

"That would mean chicken blood, wouldn't it? Easy enough to find out as long as we know what we're looking for." The Lieutenant scribbled a few notes on a sheet of paper, motioned to one of the white-jacketed chemists, passed the handkerchief to him. "I've heard about a cackle bladder, never saw one worked."

"It's an old stunt. When a mark got out of hand and looked like he might cause trouble, the con man would arrange for a gun to be handy, loaded with blanks. Then he'd needle the mark into squeezing the trigger. The con man would have a thin rubber bladder filled with chicken blood between his teeth.

When the gun goes off, he bites the bladder and the blood spurts like he's been shot full of holes."

"Sounds pretty effective."

Liddell grinned glumly. "Usually scares the mark into keeping his mouth shut and making tracks. That's for sure."

The chemist grinned. "Confidentially, Johnny, what'd he do? Sell you the Brooklyn Bridge?"

"The Queensboro. And what made me mad is I wanted that Brooklyn traffic." He glanced at his watch. "There's no way to speed that test up, Mike? It's got to take a couple of hours?"

The chemist nodded. "The test itself doesn't take long. It's the making the saline solution from the stains on the handkerchief. Once we can filter that, we put the clear solution into the capillary tubes and add some human antiserum. If it's human blood, in less than five minutes a white ring appears which keeps getting denser. If there's no precipitin reaction, it isn't human blood."

"Thanks. Will you call my office and leave word as soon as you know?"

"Sure thing." Michaelson copied down Liddell's telephone number, shook hands. He picked the test tube with the orange liquid from its stand, held it up to the light, jiggled it carefully. He seemed to have forgotten Liddell's presence before the private detective had reached the door.

At the end of the corridor, Liddell slipped into a telephone booth, dialed the number of his apartment. He drummed on the wooden support of the instrument with stubby fingers while he counted off the rings. On the fifth ring, the girl answered.

"Yes?" Her voice was low, cautious.

"This is Liddell, baby."

He could hear the soft release of her breath over the wire. "Is there anything new?"

Liddell grinned at the mouthpiece. "Not yet, but before the day is over I'm sure we'll be able to put you in the clear." He fumbled for a cigarette, hit his elbow, mumbled his disgust with the confined space. "I've established the fact that Carter was an old-time con man."

"What good does that do me?"

"Plenty. I left samples of the blood from his shirt front with the police lab. If my guess is right, that gun you shot him with was loaded with blanks."

"But you saw the blood yourself."

"Chicken blood."

"What?"

Liddell got the cigarette going, a wisp of smoke stung his eye, he opened the booth door. "It's an old con-man trick. They put a thin rubber bladder filled with chicken blood between their teeth, then needle the mark into shooting them with blanks. When they bite the bladder it looks like they're bleeding to death."

The phone was silent for a minute. "But I don't get it."

"You didn't go for his proposition, so he figured to get some mileage out of you anyhow. He was going to use your story in the next issue, but first he wanted a lot of publicity for the article."

"The kind he'd get if I tried to kill him."

"Right. He had a doctor standing by, probably some quack he had plenty on, and an abortion mill on the West Side where reporters couldn't get at him. But he'd see to it that word leaked out about what happened."

The girl's voice quivered. "He would have ruined me. Just to sell some extra copies?"

"Just to sell a couple of million extra copies, baby. For that, Murray Carter would have crucified his own mother."

"But suppose I denied it, suppose I——"

"The elevator boy saw you, the night clerk. His doctor and the nurses at the hospital would make it sound like he was dying. And you, yourself, were ready to give yourself up. You would have been playing right into his hand."

"I'm almost glad someone did kill him. A rat like that doesn't deserve to live." The line went dead for a moment. "Now what do I do?"

"Go on out to your place on the Island. Cook up a cocktail party or a dinner party or something. Be seen and act normal."

"Will you be coming?"

"I can't, baby. I've got work to do."

"But I want you to come, Johnny. I don't care about anything else. I want you to come out there with me."

"I'd like to, baby, you know that. But there's a killer around and I want to get him."

"Why? Like you said this morning, just because you stepped on a cockroach you don't have to feel any regret. He was nothing but a cockroach. I hope they never find the killer."

"We've got to, baby."

"Why?"

"For only one reason. That killer has the material Carter was holding over your head and sooner or later we're going to have to go up against him. I think it'd be better sooner than later."

"I'll see you tomorrow?"

Liddell nodded. "As soon as I get a couple of things rolling, I'll be in touch. In the meantime, just sit tight and let me handle everything."

CHAPTER 6

Bare Facts magazine maintained editorial offices at 1660 Broadway, a six-story old stone building wedged between a record store that spilled shrill music into the street at all hours of the day and night on one side, and a clothing store that specialized in heavily padded sports jackets on the other.

All day, song pluggers, musicians and publishers' representatives, impervious to the ear-shattering rhythms of the recorded music, stand clotted in little groups on the sidewalk and in the lobby. Upstairs there is a veritable rabbit warren of small one- and two-room suites occupied by small music publishers and smaller editorial offices.

Bare Facts had a two-room suite in the back of the building on the fifth floor. The outer room was dingy, dusty with tied bundles of back issues of the magazine stacked to the ceiling. There was a small desk with a typewriter of ancient vintage, un-occupied at the moment.

In the inside room, two dust-stained windows faced out on the stone wall of an areaway. A man sat at the only desk in the room, his heels hooked on the corner of the desk, his chair tilted back against the wall. His receding hairline revealed a freckled pate, bristling eyebrows gave him the appearance of constantly frowning. His skin was leathery, there was a faint glisten of silver bristles along the chin line.

He turned as Liddell walked into the room, scowled at him. "You from Carter?" He dropped his feet to the floor. "I've been trying to reach him all morning. The printer is screaming and——"

"I'm not from Carter."

The man at the desk grunted. "Then who the hell are you?"

"My name's Liddell. I'm a private detective."

The editor shook his head, waved his hand. "We're not buying any material, Liddell. We're loaded with inventory right now."

Liddell grinned glumly. "I'm not selling material. I'm looking for Carter."

The man behind the desk swabbed at his bald pate with a soiled handkerchief. "Sorry. We get a lot of private eyes wander in here trying to sell us stuff. Some of it's good, but we prefer to buy from our own sources." He stowed the handkerchief in his hip pocket, leaned back and laced his fingers at the back of his neck. "I'm Bob Hunter. I run the sheet for Carter."

"Got any idea where I can find him?"

The editor shook his head. "Like I said, I've been trying to raise him all morning. He left orders not to be disturbed, but I got a deadline to meet." He studied Liddell. "You got a beef?"

"Why?"

Hunter shrugged, grinned. "Most everybody who comes in here has. They either bust up the joint or sit around and wait to take a poke at Carter. Either way it's okay with me. I only work here."

"I might have a beef."

"It figures. Who?"

"Celeste Pierce."

The editor pursed his lips. "Nice piece of goods. What about Celeste Pierce?"

"You've got an article scheduled on her. I don't think it better run."

"Don't try to scare me, mister. It's been tried by experts. I'm not only libel proof, I'm mayhem proof. Besides, I don't remember any article on Celeste Pierce."

"Look, don't play games with me. I know the

article's scheduled for the next issue. You're the editor. So you know, too. The article doesn't run—or you'd better start."

Hunter shook his head. "You're wasting your breath. Why tell me what runs or what doesn't run? Tell Carter. He's the boss."

"I intend to. I also intend to——"

The phone on the corner of the desk jangled. The bald-headed man scooped it up. "That's him now. You can tell him all about it." He held the instrument to his ear. "Yeah, Boss. I've been—" he broke off, frowned—"Who?" The grin on his face faded, a tight look came into his eyes. "When did it happen? Yeah. I'll be up." He dropped the receiver back on its hook, stared up at Liddell. "You'll need a ouija board to tell him anything. That was the police. Carter is dead. Murdered."

"Murdered?"

"Don't look so surprised. It was bound to happen sooner or later." He reached down to the lower drawer, brought up a bottle of bourbon. "They were lining up for the honor. He just wouldn't stand still long enough."

"Who did it?"

"The cops didn't confide in me." Hunter got up, walked unsteadily over to where an ancient water cooler stood against the wall, humming to itself. He took three paper cups, filled one with water, returned to the desk. "Will you join me in a toast to my late employer who is now undoubtedly complaining about the unseasonably hot weather?"

"This should sell a lot of magazines."

The bald-headed man spilled some bourbon into two of the cups, softened it with water from the third. "If we had a magazine to sell." He looked up. "That's what the printer is screaming about. I don't have the feature for the next issue. Carter was sitting on it. He was supposed to decide by this morning."

"You don't have the feature? If you were going to run today, certainly the feature must have been set up in type? The printer must still have the type."

Hunter lifted the bourbon to his lips, tilted it. Some of the liquor ran from the corner of his mouth, dripped from his chin. "We print offset. We paste up the pages from galleys, then shoot a plate and print from that. Carter has a standing rule. He gets all galleys and original copy on futures and the type is destroyed. Like that there can't be any leaks."

Liddell pulled over a wooden chair, swung it around, straddled it. "And he had the only copy on the feature for this issue?"

"The only copy. The rest of the book is ready. All I had to do to run is paste up the feature and shoot it to the printer." He ran the flat of his hand

53

along the bristles on his chin. "You were right. That client of yours, that Celeste Pierce. She was the feature," he admitted.

"So why were you playing it cozy?"

Hunter shrugged. "Carter might have changed his mind. He'd done it before at the last minute. That's why I was so anxious to contact him. He was supposed to let me know if the article ran or not. If it did, there were some things I was supposed to do."

"Such as?"

The editor pulled open the top drawer of his desk. "I was supposed to plant this with the wire services and the city desks. Before I did, I checked the hospital he was supposed to be in. They hadn't heard from him. At the penthouse they said he couldn't be disturbed so I figured everything was off. Unless I can find the article there's no point in planting this."

Johnny Liddell picked up the typewritten sheet. It read:

> Last night, Murray Carter, publisher of *Bare Facts* magazine, was shot and seriously wounded by Celeste Pierce, glamorous redheaded movie star, over an article scheduled to appear in the forthcoming issue of the magazine.
>
> The publisher, who was admitted to West Side Private Hospital, has refused to affirm or deny the shooting but his private physician, who identified the assailant for reporters, described his

condition as too serious to permit further questioning . . .

Liddell tossed the paper back on the desk. "That thing is loaded with libel. It's a tough break for your publicity stunt but Celeste Pierce has an unbreakable alibi right up until a half hour ago."

"But if she killed him——"

Liddell snorted. "It's a publicity stunt and you know it. You plant that thing and I'll see that you're thrown into the jug on a criminal libel rap for the rest of your life. You think that doc is going to stick his neck out for you? You think that hospital isn't going to clean its skirts by admitting it was to be a phony wound?"

Hunter stared at the story morosely. "I only work here. It wasn't my idea." He indicated Liddell's drink. "You're not drinking."

"Be my guest." Liddell watched the editor pick the cup up and toss it off in a gulp. "Celeste didn't kill him. Who did, Hunter?"

The man behind the desk reached over to the radiator, picked up a copy of the Manhattan Telephone Directory, dropped it on the desk. "There's a partial list of the people who'll benefit by his death. You'll have to write my name in. I don't have a phone."

"If you didn't like the guy, why did you work for him?"

"I formed an unbreakable habit early in life—eating three meals a day." He poured some more bourbon into his glass. "You think I had a choice? Nobody takes a job like this if he could get anything else."

"You're an editor. There must be other publications that need an editor."

Hunter snorted. "I'm blackballed. From one end of the country to the other. Nobody but Carter would touch me. Not with a six foot pole."

"And now that he's dead?"

"No job lasts forever. Maybe it's a break for me. Now I can work in a nice cool sewer instead of over a red-hot typewriter." He swirled the liquor around the sides of the cup. "What do you figure will happen to the files?"

"Impounded probably. The homicide boys will probably want to go over them for possible suspects. He was pushing around a lot of people."

"A lot of people"—Hunter nodded solemnly—"a lot of tough people."

"Like?"

"Slugger Ryan, the ex-champ. We did an article on him. The one about—" he broke off, peered at Liddell—"you read *Bare Facts*?"

Liddell shook his head.

The editor tsch-tsched. "You should. Full of vital information. Who's crossing the color line, who likes his vice versa, who kicks in whose doors and for what. You can't carry on a polite social conversation without these tidbits at your fingertips."

"So I'm a social leper. What about the champ?"

"Ex-champ," Hunter rebuked. "Carter got wind of the fact that Ryan used to use his mother for a punching bag. He got one of the Ryans that hasn't talked to Slugger in years to by-line a piece about what a louse he was. Ryan didn't like it."

"It could happen."

"So anyway, Slugger comes busting in here one morning looking for Carter. He tore the place apart and then hung around the building for days waiting for Carter to show. He didn't know that the Great Man operated strictly from the penthouse."

"Who else?"

"Just read the back issues. Most of them won't be doing any mourning when the news breaks."

Liddell nodded. "Most of them will be glad to hear he's dead, but how many of them would have the nerve to do it?"

Hunter held his cup to his lips, drained it. Then he thoughtfully crushed it in his fist, tossed it at a wastebasket. "Maybe they didn't have the nerve to do it themselves. Maybe they hired a gun."

"Like me?"

"You said it, not me."

Liddell grinned crookedly. "That would be

jumping from the frying pan into the fire. Giving a pro a hold like that. Besides, once the article had appeared, the damage was done. Right?"

"You're not making out a good case for your client. Hers was on the fire. Now it probably will never appear."

"Didn't that ever happen before?"

"Once in a while. There was a crooner he had a real juicy piece on. It was skedded and set to run, but Carter ordered it killed."

"Which crooner?"

"The Teen-age Prayer, Tony DeSales. Ever heard him?"

Liddell shook his head. "I'm underprivileged."

"Sounds like a sick cow but sells records. Thousands of records. Carter had this piece all set to go and DeSales was raising all kinds of hell. Then, suddenly all is peace and light."

"What do you figure?"

"A deal. Maybe the kid agreed to help Carter with his collection. He liked to make deals like that with the right people."

"What kind of collection?"

Hunter grinned. "Carter was quite a collector. He had a real yen for things like pictures, prison records, taped tender little nothings whispered to the background of creaking springs. He was peculiarly anxious to record for posterity anything that anybody was anxious to forget."

"You think he made that kind of a deal with DeSales?"

Hunter shrugged. "Like I said, I only work here. Why don't you ask DeSales what kind of a deal he made?"

"I intend to."

"Don't let that baby face of his fool you. DeSales was doing time before he was sixteen. He's pretty handy with a cutting edge."

"That what the article was about?"

"That and a couple of rapes. Tony's quite a ripe character." The editor consulted his wrist watch. "Well, don't think it wasn't nice talking to you. But I've got to get down to the morgue and view the remains of my late benefactor. You wouldn't care to join me?"

"I've already seen a stiff."

"I'll bet." He walked over to the hatrack, picked up an old Alpine model, perched it on the back of his head. "Then, of course, talking about prospects, the possibility does exist that your client decided to get him off her back."

"Possibility, but very remote."

Hunter nodded. "Yeah, I guess it would be. In that case, there always remains the possibility that he died of old age."

CHAPTER 7

Johnny Liddell
pushed his way through the frosted glass door that
bore the legend "Johnny Liddell—Private Investigation."

The outer office was divided into two by a low
railing, behind which sat a pert little orange-haired
girl in a tight-fitting Nile-green sweater. As he entered
she looked up from the typewriter at which she was
pecking away, taking excessive care not to fracture
the finish on her nails.

Outside the railing, there was a comfortable
couch, a low table with reasonably current issues of
leading magazines. The couch was empty.

"Hi, boss," Pinky greeted him cheerfully.

He looked at the empty couch, raised his eyebrows. The redhead shrugged.

"Been trying to reach you. You had a couple of
calls."

He pushed open the gate set in the railing, walked over to her desk. "Anything important?"

"Consolidated Insurance called. You won't have to do that investigation. The widow has withdrawn the double indemnity claim." She looked up. "Do we bill them for the groundwork you did?"

Liddell nodded. "Might as well. Just to keep them honest. My guess is it was my showing up that scared the old girl into withdrawing the claim. They want to use me as a bogeyman they might as well pay."

"Check." Pinky made a note on her pad. "The only other call was from Lieutenant Michaelson at the police lab. He says it isn't human."

Liddell grunted his satisfaction.

"What was he talking about? My working conditions?"

"I left a bloodstain sample with him. I wanted to know whether or not it was human."

The redhead brightened. "You mean we're working?"

"Sure we're working. On a big one. Murray Carter."

She puzzled over the name for a moment, then her brow cleared. "You mean the guy who puts out that scandal sheet?" She pulled open her drawer, brought out a copy of the latest issue. "This Murray Carter?"

Liddell scowled at her. "So that's how you pass your time? Reading that stuff?"

Pinky grinned at him insolently. "Where do you think I get all the dirt I pass along to you?" She dropped the magazine back into the drawer, pushed it shut. "You going to do some work for Carter?"

"Not for him. On him. He's dead."

"Murdered?"

Liddell nodded.

The redhead didn't seem too impressed. "It figured. Taking other people's private lives apart is no way to break ninety, that's for sure. Who are we working for?"

"Celeste Pierce."

Pinky whistled softly. "The Rexall redhead, huh? She kill him?"

"Don't talk like that. Our clients never kill anybody."

"You could fool me. There's an awful high mortality rate among acquaintances of people we work for." She picked a blank card from the small index file, started filling it in. "Do we have a retainer or are we taking this one out in trade?"

He scowled at her, headed for the door marked "Private." On his desk there was a small pile of envelopes. The first three he dropped into the basket unopened. Two of the remaining were bills. The last one was an acknowledgment from a West Coast

62

agency for help he had rendered in a runaway case. The Coast outfit offered its co-operation in return at any time.

"Don't send thanks, send money," he grunted. He flipped the note at his wastebasket, walked over to the big window that faced out over Bryant Park. Twelve stories below, the strollers and sitters on the benches looked like little ants.

After a moment, he walked to the door, pulled it open.

"Pink, call downstairs to Acme. See if Red Daniels can run up for a few minutes. I may be able to use him."

The redhead nodded, started dialing a number with the eraser end of her pencil. Liddell closed the door, returned to his examination of the antlike creatures in Bryant Park.

He was on his second cigarette, hadn't moved from the window, when the knock came on the door. The door swung open, revealed the grinning face of a tall, lanky man with a wild shock of red hair. His face was dappled with freckles, he was addicted to outrageously loud suits. He ambled into the office with a swinging gait, dropped into the customer's chair. "You wanted to see me, Johnny?"

"Got some spare time, Red?" Johnny Liddell sat down behind the desk, tilted the desk chair back.

"Depends. I don't think you'll have any trouble

63

clearing a couple of days with the chief, but starting Monday I'll be up in Buffalo on a plant security check."

"It won't take that long." Liddell pulled a penciled list of names from his breast pocket, studied it. "I've got eight names I want a rundown on. I want to know which of the eight was in town last night and if they weren't could they have sneaked in and out. Can do?"

"Depends. If it's Minnie Zilch of Keokuk, might be tough. If it's somebody who leaves a trace, can do."

Liddell leaned his forearms on the desk, reached for a pack of cigarettes. He shook two loose, tossed one to the redhead. "It's the kind that leaves a trace."

"Like for instance?"

Liddell consulted the list. "Laurie Evans, Slugger Ryan, Sonny Morris."

The red-haired man touched a lighter to his cigarette, filled his lungs with smoke. He fumbled through his pockets, came up with a folded sheet of paper and a pencil. "Let's take them slow. What was that first one?"

"Laurie Evans. She sings with Del Cort's band."

Red Daniels nodded. "Let's have the rest."

"Slugger Ryan you know. Tony DeSales you know. He's the crooner."

The redhead nodded, grimaced to keep the

smoke out of his eyes. "Sonny Morris, you mentioned. He's the hood?"

"Right." Liddell underscored a name on the list with his thumb nail. "Zora Marissoff, she's some kind of a Georgian princess or something, strictly Social Register. So is Tim Carpenter."

"You want him, too?"

"Him, Leo Dugan the fight promoter and Mike Regan the English actor." He folded the envelope, dropped it on the top of the desk, watched as the other man puzzled over the list.

"Do I get to ask questions?"

Liddell grinned. "Like you always say. Depends."

"What's the connection between this assortment? Hollywood, the Social Register, Madison Square Garden and the mob."

"Maybe none. Maybe there's a killer in there. Think you can get it for me by this evening?"

The redhead ran his eyes over the list, nodded. "Should be able to. Most of them can be checked through Celebrity Service, the rest we can pin down with a couple of wires." He folded the paper, stuck it into his pocket. "You kidding about maybe there's a killer in here? This doesn't sound like that kind of material."

"All of them have a good motive for the kill."

"Whose kill?"

Liddell took the cigarette from between his lips, blew a stream of smoke at the glowing end. "Murray Carter. The guy who publishes that scandal rag."

Red Daniels grunted. "Heard about that in a late flash on WNEW." He ran the tips of his fingers along the sides of his jaw. "Why only eight?"

"I have a hunch that the killer is more likely to be someone who's been trying to stall an article that hasn't appeared rather than someone who's already been crucified. Once the article appears, you might be mad. But not killing mad."

"And these?"

"Subjects of future articles. Ryan, for instance, is about to get the treatment for the second time. Tony DeSales was supposed to get it, but for some reason it was called off. Maybe Carter changed his mind and decided to go ahead with it. The others are all ready to run."

"And you think one of these would be willing to kill to stop it?"

"It could be." He unfolded the envelope, checked the notation next to each name. "Any one of them would be ruined by the stuff Carter had on them. You can get awful desperate when you get pushed into that kind of corner."

"Where do you fit in all this, Johnny?"

Liddell picked up a pencil, doodled on the top sheet of his desk pad. "I've got a client on it."

"One of these?"

Liddell looked up, shook his head. "I don't need a check on my client. I know where she was all night. With me."

Red Daniels grinned lewdly. "The old Liddell service. Alibis furnished night and day."

Liddell started to retort when the door to the private office burst open. A man filled the doorway. He was big all over from the bulging shoulders to the hamlike fists. He was wearing a rumpled blue suit and hadn't bothered to take the grey fedora off his head.

"I tried to tell him you were busy," Pinky protested across the big man's shoulder, "but this big ape just pushed his way in."

Liddell's eyes roamed from the thick shoulders to the heavily soled shoes that practically wore a badge.

"Be with you in a minute, mac," he grunted. "If you don't mind waiting outside until——"

"I don't mind nothing, shamus. But the inspector minds being kept waiting. He wants to see you. Now." His expressionless grey eyes jumped from Liddell to Red Daniels and back. "When he says now, he means right now."

"What's it all about?" Liddell scowled.

"He didn't say," the plainclothesman told him placidly.

Liddell growled under his breath, turned back to Red Daniels. "As soon as you have anything for me, call it in. I'll be in touch." He watched while the redheaded man pulled himself out of the chair, headed for the door. "Look, I suppose you know it's not legal to go around busting into people's offices, pushing them around?"

"Neither is murder, shamus. Let's go. In case I forgot to tell you, the inspector don't like to be kept waiting."

CHAPTER 8

The police sedan stopped in front of the low stone building that houses the morgue at Bellevue Hospital. It is set back from the river and neither the hum of traffic along the nearby East River Drive nor the clank of barges nor the occasional hoot of a tug penetrates its thick, damp walls. Even if they did, they wouldn't disturb the deep slumber of its occupants.

The plainclothesman opened the door on his side, waited until Johnny Liddell had joined him. They walked to the heavy metal door, pushed it open, grimaced at the heavy, tangible smell of death that spilled out at them. An elevator whined to a stop on the floor as they entered the short corridor. An attendant in a white jacket slammed back the old-fashioned iron grillwork door and wheeled out a stretcher. A body was strapped to it. Today was shipping day and it was on its way on its last trip to Potter's Field in an unmarked pine box.

Liddell and the plainclothesman stepped aside as it was wheeled past, entered the elevator. It grunted and groaned its way down to the basement refrigerating vault where the air is heavy with dampness. The smell of disinfectants and the pervading odor of death assailed their nostrils.

The plainclothesman tapped him on the shoulder, led Liddell to the small office and receiving room where fresh arrivals are prepared for the vault. A group of men were huddled around a suggestively shaped bulge on the sandstone examining table. One of the men was Inspector Herlehy of Homicide.

He glared at the private detective as the plainclothesman stepped up to him, whispered into his ear. The inspector nodded, the man in the rumpled blue suit touched his finger to the brim of the fedora, stepped back and headed back to the elevator.

"Nice of you to come, Liddell," Herlehy grunted.

"You mean I had a choice? That character busted into my office, chased a client and practically dragged me down here."

"I'll have to talk to him about that," the inspector told him.

"I'll bet." He looked past the inspector to the canvas-covered bulge. "Anyone I know?"

"That's one of the things I wanted to ask you." Herlehy nodded to the attendant, waited until he had caught the end of the heavy canvas, pulled it back. "Is it?"

Murray Carter lay on his back, staring at the overhead light with eyes that would never see again. His hair was wet, dank and washed back from his face. His neck was supported by a notched wooden block.

"Looks like a character named Murray Cartman. An old-time con man."

Inspector Herlehy spat out an old wad of gum into the wastebasket, denuded a fresh piece, stuck it between his teeth. "This is Murray Carter, publisher of *Bare Facts*. And you know it." He chomped on the fresh piece of gum.

"I also know it's Murray Cartman, a con man." He picked up the limp hand of the dead man, saw the stains of the inking pad. "You'll know it, too, as soon as you get a make on those prints."

Herlehy looked thoughtful. "You leveling with me?"

"I always level with you, Inspector. This character has a record for extortion as long as your arm."

The inspector nodded for the attendant to cover the body. "Is that why you wanted to see him this morning?"

"Did I?"

Herlehy growled at him. "His editor, Bob Hunter, says you did. That is, if you didn't already know he was dead."

"How would I know that?"

The inspector stared at him, let it pass. "What did you want to see him about this morning?"

"It was on a client's business."

"What client?"

Liddell grinned at him glumly. "You know I'm not at liberty to discuss that, Inspector."

"Look, Liddell"—the inspector's voice was deceptively soft—"this is a murder investigation, not a May party. You show up looking for a man with a beef and later that man shows up dead. I add that up and I get trouble. Trouble I can do without. What did you want to see Carter about?"

"My client had been tipped off he was going to run a libelous piece about her. I wanted to tip him off that she wouldn't take it sitting down."

"Tip him off how? With a slug through the back of his head?"

Liddell considered it. He looked around. The other men had withdrawn a short distance, stared at him with no show of expression. "You have any reason to say I killed him, Inspector?"

"You've been known to get overzealous in protecting a client. This time you might have gone all out."

Liddell pursed his lips, managed to look serious. "What time is he supposed to have been killed?"

Herlehy nodded to one of the men, who whipped a notebook from his pocket. "The body was discovered by a maid at twelve forty-five P.M. Pending autopsy, the M.E. sets it anywhere between midnight and five A.M."

"Pretty wide area of time to account for," Liddell complained mildly.

"Maybe not. We may be able to narrow it down. Carter was alive at four forty. He took a phone call from the night clerk," Herlehy snapped. "I suppose you were in bed alone at that time?"

Liddell grinned. "That's a rather indelicate question inasmuch as I was with a lady at that time. Had been since before three as a matter of fact."

"You can prove that?" Herlehy growled.

"If I have to. A lady like my client couldn't come into a place like my hotel at three and not make an impression. Although the desk clerk is ordinarily very discreet, I'm sure he could be prevailed upon to tell you what time she arrived."

There was a tight expression around the inspector's eyes. "Your client? How convenient. She alibis you and you alibi her. Who is this client?"

Liddell shook his head. "I'd rather not say."

A plainclothesman came out of a little office off the examining room, walked over to the inspector and whispered into his ear. Herlehy looked from the newcomer to Liddell and back.

"You stay here," he snapped at Liddell. "I'll be right back." He headed for the small office, slammed the door behind him.

When he returned, his face was stained an angry red, his jaws were beating a merciless tattoo on the gum. He stopped in front of Liddell, jutted his jaw out at him.

"When are you going to stop trying to play games with this department?"

"Such as?"

"What do you think we're running here, a police department or a home for backward flatfeet?"

The low conversation among the other men had stopped, they stood listening to the inspector.

"And if I say I don't know what you're talking about?"

"I'm talking about a handkerchief you left with Michaelson this morning. He ran a check for you on the stains on it. Is that right?"

Liddell nodded.

"Coincidentally enough, the tech boys who worked over Carter's flat also forwarded some sample bloodstains taken from the dead man's shirt front. Michaelson has just reported that they match the stains on the handkerchief you brought in."

74

"Is there any law against having a handkerchief stained with chicken blood?"

Herlehy glared at him. The red was beginning to recede from his face and neck. "I just told you the stains match the blood on Carter's shirt."

"So the stains on Carter's shirt were chicken blood too. I also told you that Carter has a record this long as a con man and extortionist. Doesn't that add up to something?"

Herlehy looked thoughtful. "A cackle bladder?"

"What then? Carter used that old one to cool off someone who was steamed over an article he was going to run. That someone was my client"—he took a deep breath—"that's how I got the stained handkerchief. You know the way a bladder like that is liable to spurt. She got some on her hands and wiped them off on a handkerchief she picked up from his desk. But he was alive over an hour after she left if your timing is correct."

Herlehy looked around, grunted. "Let's go inside and get this straightened away." He started toward the small office off the examining room.

It was furnished with a small enameled metal desk, some filing cabinets and two chairs. The inspector hoisted one hip on the corner of the desk, waited until Liddell had closed the door after him. "Okay. Now level with me, Liddell, or I'll pull your ticket so fast it'll burn a hole through your pocket."

Liddell held up a pack of cigarettes, drew a nod. "My client is a big movie star. If her name has to come into it, I'll tell you. I'd rather not."

"Let's have it."

Liddell managed to look unhappy. He touched a match to the cigarette, drew a lungful of smoke. "Celeste Pierce. She's the hottest thing in pictures today."

Herlehy chewed at his gum thoughtfully. "Go on."

"She called me in to represent her in buying back some exposé material on her past. Last night Carter got to her, told her if she didn't stooge for him by fingering other stars for his magazine he was going to print the story and give her the full treatment."

"So?"

"She refused. He was ready for that, too. She was going to be useful to him one way or the other. If she played ball, he'd use her to bird-dog material. If she didn't, he'd put her in a spot where she'd sell millions of copies for him."

"By pretending she shot him. That what you think?"

"That's what I know. The gun was laying right where she could get it. The whole business smells of the cackle bladder setup."

Herlehy raked his fingers through his hair. "You're just guessing."

Liddell shook his head. "This morning, that stooge of his showed me an article he was supposed to plant with the papers as soon as he got the go-ahead from Carter. It told how my client tried to kill Carter to keep the story about her from appearing." He watched the inspector's face. "We can prove it wasn't my client, but even so she can still be hurt."

"How?"

"The material he was going to use in the magazine is still at Carter's apartment."

Herlehy shook his head. "There's nothing there that's worth a damn. Somebody cleaned out his files, took everything that might be worth something."

Liddell managed to look concerned. "There can be an awful lot of heat generated by a deal like this, Inspector. A lot of innocent people can get hurt. And the studios aren't going to stand still and let somebody destroy properties they've got fortunes invested in."

"That thought has occurred to me. But there's not a helluva lot we can do about it. Or maybe you have a suggestion?"

"You won't like it."

"That's for sure. Let's have it anyway."

Liddell smoked for a moment. "If the department starts digging into Carter's operation, it's going to uncover a lot of sensational stuff and the news-papers are going to have a picnic. Anything you dig is public property—and you're going to get fingered for every big name that gets dragged through the mud."

"I'll live through it."

"But why live through it if you can duck it? Look, we're not one hundred per cent sure he was killed because of his magazine. It could have been an old victim or an attempted snatch or even a stickup. The police will have to look into those possibilities, won't they?"

Herlehy chewed deliberately, nodded.

"Okay. While you're covering those angles, give me a free hand to screen all the possibilities among the people he crucified in that rag of his."

The white-haired man shook his head. "I can't do it."

"Just seventy-two hours, Inspector. I may not come up with the killer, but I can probably eliminate a lot of big names for you."

"Why would you be so willing to do that?"

Liddell grinned a tight smile. "The killer has that material on my client. I'd consider it a fee to get it back unopened."

"And the other material that's missing? Hunter says there were over a dozen articles awaiting publi-cation that are apparently missing."

"I turn them over to the D.A. to be destroyed."

Herlehy raked his fingers through his hair in indecision. "I couldn't take the responsibility for it, Johnny. I'll put it up to the D.A. and see what he has to say. If it's okay with him, it's okay with my division."

"The heat from this one could easily shrivel his chances of ever moving up to Albany. There's an awful lot of big names involved."

"Don't tell me about it. Save it for him. The only thing Albany means to me is that I'm halfway to my lodge on Lake George."

CHAPTER 9

The district attorney's
office is in the Criminal Courts Building. It consists
of a series of small offices for the assistants to the
district attorney and large, more elegantly furnished
quarters for the D.A. himself.

Each of the assistants' offices has an antechamber with chairs for prospective witnesses, each has a
series of doors so that witnesses can be maneuvered
from office to office without coming face to face with
other witnesses.

Inspector Herlehy deposited Johnny Liddell in
the antechamber of the assistant assigned to homicide. The homicide section of the district attorney's
office is a completely separate unit with complete
facilities for handling the investigation, preparation
and actual trial of homicides. The assistant in charge
of the homicide section is usually regarded as the
heir apparent to the district attorney himself since

most of the publicity-worthy cases fall into his lap.

Mark Jacobs, in charge of the Homicide Bureau, was painfully aware of the probability of his accession and had played his cards close to the vest in order to assure it.

He was a product of City College, a school where only the fittest survived with thousands clamoring for the free education that could only be made available to hundreds. He had come out in 1932, in the heart of the depression, knew what it meant to stand on line hours for a sales clerk's job that had been advertised the night before. He had gotten his law degree at St. Johns and had put in his time night in and night out at the 23rd A.D. until it was his time to hit the leader for an appointment.

Slowly, doggedly, he had worked his way from the Indictment Bureau in the D.A.'s office to the coveted plum of chief of the Homicide Bureau. A day never passed that he didn't detour past the big double doors that opened on the Old Man's office so that he could see in his mind's eye a gleaming brass plaque on the door that read "Marcus A. Jacobs, District Attorney." Every day that passed, he knew, he was one day closer to that big day.

And now, when things seemed to be going so well, Inspector Herlehy had dropped a hot one into his lap. From the scant outline the inspector had given him, Mark Jacobs knew that the Murray Carter murder was loaded with political dynamite. He also knew that the Old Man would dump it back into his lap when he, too, recognized the short fuse on it.

"You say his client is Celeste Pierce?" he asked Herlehy.

The inspector nodded. "She's just one of the names that are bound to spill if we start digging, Mark." He crushed the wad of gum between his powerful jaws. "You know the way Carter operated. He used only names. Big names."

The assistant D.A. grunted. "Too big." He got out of his chair, paced the room, hands clasped behind his back, head slightly bowed. "You think Liddell can screen out the ones who had no connection with it?"

Herlehy considered. "He's a good man," he allowed. "He may have a couple of private angles. But he says he'll level with us. I'm inclined to go along with him."

Jacobs stopped his pacing alongside his desk, pounded absently on it with clenched fist. "It's a helluva note when the Police Department and the D.A.'s office have to call in a private eye." He looked up at the inspector. "What do you think the newspapers would do to us if it got out?"

"No more than the studios and some of the society people involved will do if it spills over into the newspapers."

"They didn't do anything to Carter. They couldn't stop him from publishing the stuff."

Herlehy looked glum. "Someone did."

The assistant D.A. waved the objection aside impatiently. "I mean the rest. The ones that didn't kill him."

"He didn't have a political future. And he wasn't on the city payroll," Herlehy grunted. "It's okay with me. You say turn my men loose to dig whatever Carter was getting ready to spill, I'll do it."

"Wait a minute." Jacobs walked wearily to his chair, dropped into it. He puffed his cheeks, blew his breath out in a silent whistle. "A couple of days can't make that much difference." He picked up a pencil, doodled on the yellow pad on his desk. "As I understand it, Liddell wants seventy-two hours to work on the possibles in the case who were crucified by Carter." He waited for a nod from the inspector. "You're going to leak the information that the killing was an attempted snatch or stick-up that went wrong and tackle it from that end?"

"For seventy-two hours. By the end of that time, Liddell will have gone through Carter's back issues and futures and eliminated the necessity for us to drag some of those red-hots in here."

Jacobs nodded. "It might take some of the heat off," he conceded. "The newsboys are going to stick awful close to our boys. Any attempt to question any of those people officially will start fireworks."

"Want to talk to Liddell?"

"I guess we might as well."

Herlehy walked to the door of the office opening on the antechamber. Johnny Liddell was comfortable on a chair, exchanging reminiscences with George Daly, a detective assigned to Jacobs's office.

"Want to come in, Johnny?" Herlehy called to him.

Liddell slapped the detective on the shoulder, walked over to where Herlehy stood with the door open. He walked in, found Mark Jacobs chewing on the rubber eraser on his pencil. The right side of his desk was filled with stacks of foolscap, legal size. The assistant D.A. was doing a bad job of pretending to be absorbed in one. He put it aside as Liddell walked in.

"Sit down, Liddell." He waved to a chair across the desk from himself. "The inspector says you have some ideas on the Carter killing. Naturally, we're always interested in ideas."

"Naturally," Liddell agreed dryly.

The D.A. raised his eyebrows, looked from Liddell to the inspector. "I thought Liddell wanted to co-operate?"

"I do. But with all cards on the table, Mr. Jacobs," Liddell told him. "I have a stake in finding the killer as fast as possible. You have a stake in finding him without a lot of dirty linen being aired in the newspapers. Neither one of us is doing the other a favor. If that's the way you understand it, too, then we can work together."

Jacobs chewed on the end of his pencil. "I understand your client Celeste Pierce isn't in too good a position on this one," he reminded the private detective gently.

"Her position's all right. You could give her a bad time," he conceded. "But that studio she's under contract to has a lot of money invested in her. If they got the idea you were deliberately crucifying her to get your name in the paper, they might get awful mad."

"And if we can pin something on her?"

Liddell shook his head. "You can't. She's got an ironclad alibi. You might be able to prove Carter was getting ready to smear her in his rag and that she was up there last night to talk him out of it. But all that would do would be to wreck an investment Pyramid Pictures has sunk a lot of money into."

Jacobs looked to the inspector.

Herlehy nodded. "The Pierce girl left before three according to the elevator boy and the clerk. Carter was taking a telephone call at four thirty." He nodded to Liddell. "She went into his place at a little after three, left late this morning."

The D.A. looked at Liddell with interest. "Nice

work if you can get it. Do you give all your clients that personal service?"

"Only if they're female."

Jacobs tossed the pencil back on the desk. "All right, I think we're willing to make a deal. You get seventy-two hours to screen out the possibles who might have gotten mad enough to kill Carter for what he did to them in his magazine. You keep us informed of whom you've contacted and what you've found."

Liddell considered it, nodded.

"You got any ideas, Liddell?" Herlehy wanted to know.

"I'll have more after I put on a pair of hip boots and wade through some of the filth in his back issues."

"You think that's where you'll find the killer?"

Liddell rubbed the side of his nose irritably. "No. As a matter of fact, I don't. By now most of the damage he could do those people has been done. There's only one in that batch who might hold a grudge long enough to kill him."

"Who's that?" Jacobs asked cautiously.

"Slugger Ryan, the ex-champ."

The D.A. groaned audibly. "Slugger Ryan?" He looked to Herlehy. "Isn't he owned by Leo Dugan?"

The inspector nodded.

"Take it easy with the Slugger if you can, Liddell. Leo Dugan has a half a dozen Tammany leaders in his pocket. He's up to his hips in politics."

Liddell grinned. "That's why I figured it would be easier for them to get mad at me than at you."

"Why do you pick out the Slugger, Liddell?" Herlehy wanted to know.

"He busted up the *Bare Facts* office and hung around for days trying to get a crack at Carter after the first article. I have a tip that Carter was going to rub more salt in the wound in a second article documented with proof that Ryan went into the tank on his last fight—at Leo Dugan's orders."

Jacobs groaned again.

"If neither Dugan nor the Slugger killed Carter, what happens to those articles and the proofs?"

"That's part of the deal, Mark," Herlehy told the man behind the desk. "Liddell's idea is that the killer has all this material, including the stuff on his client. He delivers the entire batch to your office——"

"Except the package on my client."

Herlehy nodded. "Except the package on his client."

The assistant D.A. resumed chewing on the pencil. "Sounds all right with me, I guess."

"You going to clear it with the Old Man?" Herlehy wanted to know.

The man behind the desk shook his head. "No need for both of us to get ulcers." He split the pencil with his teeth, tossed it at the wastebasket. "It's not bad enough we'll have those Hollywood bastards on our neck—but Tammany, yet!"

Herlehy chewed silently for a moment. "You understand, Liddell, that this is strictly unofficial. You step on any toes or get in any corners and you're on your own."

"I'll be the soul of discretion, Inspector."

The white-haired man rolled his eyes ceilingward. "This I have got to see!"

CHAPTER 10

The pungent odor of perspiration spiked with rubbing alcohol stung Johnny Liddell's nostrils as he walked in off Eighth Avenue, started up the stairs to Millton's Gym. At the head of the stairs, he dropped a coin into the turnstile, pushed through.

The walls had been broken out of what was apparently the top floor of two adjoining buildings, made into one huge room. He stood for a moment listening to the rhythmic tap dance of the punching bags, the deep grunts of the heavy bags as the hopefuls worked out on the perimeter of the ring.

In the center of the floor, a shaded bulb spilled light into a ring. It was surrounded on all four sides by camp chairs, occupied by silent men who chewed unlit cigars, watched the two men in the center of the ring. Occasionally, they might grunt, then nod. Mostly, they chewed on cigars.

In the ring, a coffee-colored Negro was dancing around his opponent, spattering him with sharp jabs. The other boy was a run-of-the-mill sparring partner, a chopping block good only to sharpen the timing and the punches of his betters.

Liddell stood at the back of the camp chairs, waited for his eyes to adjust to the semigloom. When the bell sounded for the end of the short round, he picked his way through the chairs, slid into an empty seat next to Tommy Lewis of the *Dispatch*.

Lewis was a short, dumpy man who affected wild hand-painted ties and always smelled of menthol. His by-line had once been a proud adornment to the pages of the nation's top newspapers in the form of a syndicated column, but a forced retirement of several years occasioned by a bout with acute alcoholism had relegated him to a sports assignment with the *Dispatch*. Now he worked under a sports editor who had been a copy boy in the days of Tommy's greatness.

The menthol tube had replaced the bottle and most of his acquaintances could locate the sports writer in the dark from his smell. Liddell wrinkled his nose as the odor assailed his nostrils, waited while the sports writer dug his hand into his jacket pocket, came up with a glass tube, took a deep sniff. "Be my guest?" he offered the menthol tube to Liddell.

"No, thanks. My eyes are watering from just sitting here."

"Flattery will get you no place," Lewis told him. "Besides, if you don't like the smells around here what are you doing off your beat? I thought you worked the chorus girl side."

"It smells better on that side, that's for sure," Liddell grinned. He nodded to the corner where the coffee-colored boy was being worked over. "Looks real good. Who does he belong to?"

"Leo Dugan. Who else?" He sniffed again at the menthol tube, replaced it in his pocket. "He's strictly a gym fighter. Looks real good against a stumble-bum like this, but he has no punch and no guts when he goes up against competition."

"But?"

Lewis shrugged. "But he gets to be champ anyway one of these days. Like I said, he belongs to Leo Dugan."

"Leo around?"

The sports man studied him with curiosity. "He never shows down here. What's with you and Dugan?"

"Just words. I've got a couple of ideas I wanted to talk over with him." His eyes made a circuit of the room, checking the heavyweights at the big bags. "Slugger Ryan around?"

The sports writer snorted. "This is a gym, man, not a night club. The champ doesn't train in gyms. He trains on blondes and champagne."

"The ex-champ, you mean."

Lewis winked. "Not after the next fight. It's his turn to get it back." He lowered his voice. "If you want to make a couple of bucks, get on him. It's in the bag." He cast a desultory glance toward the ring where the coffee-colored boy was going through some complicated footwork in his corner. "Ever since Sugar Ray makes himself a bundle tap dancing in some upholstered sewer, all these stumblebums feel they got to make like Gene Kelly."

Liddell nodded. "You wouldn't know where I could find the Slugger, would you?"

"First Leo Dugan, now the Slugger. Starting when are you so interested in the fight mob?"

"You read anything but the sports columns?"

Lewis considered, nodded. "Yeah. The obituary page. Not that I figure to bump into anybody I know, but I look at the ages. Some days I figure I'm away ahead. You know?"

"Then you must have heard that Murray Carter, the guy who published *Bare Facts*, has been murdered."

The sports writer nodded, grunted. "Yeah. He knocked the average away down. He was only fifty." He fished for the menthol tube again, ignored

Liddell's groan. "Can't help it, friend. Keeps the sinuses clear."

"You didn't tell me where I could find the Slugger."

Lewis inserted the tube in his right nostril, held the left and breathed deeply. Then he repeated the procedure on the other side. "You ought to try it. Clears your head real good."

"The Slugger," Liddell reminded him.

"What's the Slugger got to do with Carter getting himself knocked off?"

Liddell shrugged. "Maybe nothing. But he was gunning for Carter after *Bare Facts* did that piece on him. I just wanted to talk to him about it."

"That was a lousy piece"—Lewis shook his head— "The guy that wrote that didn't know any more about writing than I do about plumbing."

"The Slugger didn't care too much for it, either. But it wasn't its literary quality that bothered him." He waited patiently while the sports writer dabbed at the tip of his nose with a balled handkerchief. "Where can I find him, Tommy?"

"He's got a babe dances at the Cash Box on 54th. You know the place? Real clipperoo." He looked a little wistful. "Not that I get around to the joints like I used to. The sinus, you know."

Liddell nodded. "This babe. She got a name?"

"There's no grief in this for the kid, is there?

The Slugger's a three dollar bill in my book, but this kid is okay. I wouldn't want you to go bugging her."

"There's no grief in it for her. I may be able to do her a favor."

"Peddle your sex life someplace else. She's already taken."

"Look, all I want to do is get to the Slugger before the police do. They might drag her into it. I won't."

Tommy Lewis considered. "I know you got a rep for never crossing a pal. I hope you're not going to make an exception in my case."

"I give you my word she doesn't get hurt in any way."

"Okay. She calls herself Lorna Varden. She has a pad on East 63rd. Three hundred eighty-two East, an old brownstone." He laid his hand on Liddell's arm. "You know why I don't want her hurt? The kid's real name is Alice Myers. Thought Lorna Varden sounded fancier. You know? Remember Al Myers? Used to be on the *Mail?*"

"His kid?"

Lewis nodded. "So make sure she don't get hurt." He turned his attention to the ring as the heavy-shouldered sparring partner went to the floor. "Slipped," he grunted. "That fancy dancing bum couldn't flatten a cornstalk in a tornado." As the sparring partner pulled himself to his feet, shuffled toward the slimmer boy, Lewis turned back to Liddell. "You think maybe Leo and the Slugger are mixed up in the kill?"

Liddell grinned. "Look, buddy boy, you stick to the sports side. There you know your way around. You start trying to buck that high powered competition on the city side and you're likely to find out you don't look good in ulcers."

As Liddell was heading for the exit, there was an excited murmur from the group clustered around the ring. He turned to see that the sparring partner had dumped the cocoa-colored boy on the seat of his tights. Nobody looked more shocked than the sparring partner.

CHAPTER 11

Apartment houses
hadn't yet invaded this block in the East Sixties. A
row of uniform brownstones ran the length of the
street, except down near the corner of Third where
they gave way to some five-story buildings with stores
at the street level and flats above.

Lorna Varden lived in the fourth house from the
First Avenue corner on the south side of the street.
Johnny Liddell ambled up the low stoop, walked into
the dim coolness of the vestibule. It smelled of old
wood, old cooking and dampness.

A double row of highly polished brass letter
boxes gleamed on the far wall. He ran his index finger
along the cards under the boxes, stopped at one that
said simply "Varden." Beneath it was penciled the
notation "2 E."

He pressed the button, waited. When there was
no response, he rang again. On the third ring, the

latch on the hall door started to stutter, the door swung partly open.

He climbed the stairs to the second floor, followed a well-worn carpet to 2 E, knocked.

"Who is it? You, Slugger?" The voice was low, throaty.

"I've got to see you. It's about the Slugger."

"Who are you?"

Liddell sighed. "Look, Lorna. I've got to talk to you about the Slugger. If you want me to discuss your business through a closed door so everyone in the damn house can hear, that's okay with me. It may not be with you."

The door opened a crack, he felt rather than saw the eye that was applied to the opening. "What do you want?"

"Murray Carter was murdered this morning. That mean anything to you?"

He could hear the hiss of her indrawn breath, then the door swung open. She stood aside, let him enter. "Who are you?"

"My name's Liddell. I'm a private cop." He walked through the little foyer into a living room darkened by drawn shades.

The girl stood with her back to the closed door. "Is it true about Carter?"

"Don't you ever listen to the radio? It's been on the news since just after noon."

"I didn't get in until about nine this morning. I've been in bed ever since." She followed him into the room.

She was short, a chorus pony size, came up to Liddell's chin. Her thick, blonde hair hung down over her shoulders, was caught behind the ears with a blue ribbon. Her face gleamed in the half light, looked to be washed clean of all make-up.

"So Carter's dead. What do you want with the Slugger?"

"I want to talk to him before the cops do. If he had nothing to do with it, I can save him and you a lot of bad publicity."

The blonde walked past him to a window, ran up the shade, blinked at the brightness of the light. She had pulled her silk dressing gown tightly around her. Her hips worked smoothly at the fabric as she walked. When she turned around, the effect was equally interesting.

"Why should the cops want to talk to the Slugger?"

"Murder."

The girl winced. "He didn't kill anybody." She walked to an end table, helped herself to a cigarette. "I'm not sorry Carter got it, but the Slugger had nothing to do with it."

"How do you know?"

She touched a match to the cigarette. "I know the Slugger. He's not a killer."

"You could fool a lot of people. He busted up the furniture at Carter's office."

"But he didn't hurt anybody."

Liddell grinned. "Because he couldn't lay his hands on Carter. Maybe he finally caught up with him." He watched the girl pace restlessly. "The Slugger picks you up every night. Did he pick you up last night?"

"Yes."

"What time?"

"We always finish the last show at two-thirty. Slugger was there waiting. There are a dozen people who can swear to that." She smoked in short, nervous puffs.

"You came right home?"

She started to answer, bit her lip. "I already told you I didn't get home until nine."

"Slugger with you all the time?"

She glared at him. "We didn't leave the Cash Box at two-thirty. The director called a rehearsal of next week's show. We broke up about seven-thirty."

"The Slugger sat through it?"

The blonde caught her lower lip between her teeth, chewed on it, finally shook her head. "No. He got bored and walked out on us."

"What time was that?"

Lorna ground her cigarette out angrily. "How do I know? Maybe three or three-thirty." She looked up at Liddell. "What time was——"

"Sometime around in there. It means your boy was on the loose with enough time to get over and square things with Carter for what he wrote about him."

"I tell you the Slugger didn't kill anybody. He talks a lot and he brawls a lot, but he's no killer," the girl flared. "You're like all the rest of the cops. You have to find somebody to pin it on. Well, if everybody that had a reason to kill that rat got picked up you wouldn't have a jail big enough to hold them."

"You know someone else?"

"Me," the girl snapped. "I'm glad he's dead. I almost wish I could have. You think the job he did on the Slugger only hurt him? How about the people who love him, like me—or the people who have an investment in him? Don't you think they get hurt, too?"

There was the sound of a key in the lock. The color drained from the girl's face, she tried to swallow her clenched fist.

"My God, that's the Slugger now!"

Johnny Liddell swung around in time to see a bulky-shouldered man in his late twenties filling the doorway. He had never seen Slugger Ryan in his street clothes, had never realized the breadth of his shoulders, the length of his arms.

Ryan was an inverted triangle, his broad shoulders tapering down to the apex of his waist. His hair was cut in crew cut style, a heavy shadow of beard blurred the square lines of his jaw. His eyes jumped from Liddell to the girl and back, he growled something deep in his throat.

He moved fast for a big man. The door had hardly slammed behind him before he was on top of Liddell. He threw a high left that brought the private detective off balance, sank his right almost to the cuff in Liddell's midsection.

Dimly, Liddell heard the girl scream, was too busy trying to back pedal to pay any attention. Ryan kept moving in, flat-footed, both fists flailing. Liddell thought he saw an opening, threw a punch, landed high on the Slugger's cheek. Ryan bellowed his rage, moved in.

A hard right to the jaw half spun Liddell around, started bells ringing in his head. The Slugger caught him by the shoulder, swung him back around and met him flush with a straight overhand that knocked him back over an end table. He landed on the floor in the debris, didn't move.

It seemed a long time before consciousness came knocking at the back of Liddell's skull. He opened his eyes, looked up into the worried face of the blonde girl. He felt the welcome wetness of the cloth she laid across his forehead, permitted her to wipe away a thin red stream that ran from the corner of his mouth.

"I thought you were never going to come to," Lorna sighed her relief.

"Where is he?" Liddell growled thickly. "Where's Ryan?"

"He's gone."

Liddell touched the tender spot on the side of his jaw gingerly, explored the cut on the inside of his lip. "That boy friend of yours plays real rough," he grumbled. He tried to sit up, groaned and sank back.

"I should have warned you. He's terribly jealous. That's why he picks me up every night after the show."

Liddell made a second try at sitting up, managed to make it this time. "Now she tells me."

"This time you really couldn't blame him. It did look pretty bad, I guess, to come in and find me dressed like this and entertaining a man." She caught him under the arm, helped him to his feet where he stood swaying. "An attractive man at that."

"If you like the battered type," he grunted. He leaned against the wall until a feeling of nausea passed. "Where is he?"

The blonde shook her head stubbornly. "I don't know."

"If you did, would you tell me?"

She shook her head again.

"That's what I thought. In that case, I'll give you something to tell him. Tell him to do himself a favor and give himself up. Tell him it'd be a lot better for everybody if he finds me before I find him."

"I told him what you wanted. He said he didn't have anything to do with Murray Carter getting himself killed. He doesn't want to get mixed up in it."

"My heart bleeds for him." He touched a handkerchief to his battered lip, brought it away pink stained. "And that ain't all."

Leo Dugan directed the affairs of the Continental Boxing Club from an air-conditioned office in the Madison Square Club Building. He had built the legend that he had no secretary because he needed no buffer between himself and his friends. A facetious sports columnist had a different interpretation—that Mrs. Leo Dugan had forbidden him to have a female any place in his office.

He was bull-necked, heavy-set. He had the ruddy complexion that comes from juicy steaks, aged bourbon and expert massages. His hair was parted geometrically in the center, flattened down on his skull.

A fine tracing of blue veins in his nose had failed to react to care, gave a touch of W. C. Fields to his appearance.

His voice was raspy, harsh. He stared at Johnny Liddell unsympathetically. "So the Slugger dropped you. What'd you expect him to do? Throw his arms around you?"

Liddell ran the tips of his fingers along his jaw. "Look, I didn't come up here to cry on your shoulder. I can take care of the Slugger in my own way. Right now, I'm trying to find out if he saw Carter last night?"

Dugan buffed his nails on the rough texture of his sports jacket, admired them. "And I told you that the Slugger hasn't been near that creep and his office in weeks." He looked up. "Not that I'd blame him if he tore that rat apart." He dropped his eyes. "But he didn't."

"Carter did quite a job on him in that magazine."

The promoter nodded. "That was a couple of months ago. You think anybody remembers what was in last month's magazine, or yesterday's paper?" He picked up a letter opener fashioned in the shape of a scimitar. "You got the guy wrong. He's no killer outside the ring."

Liddell grunted. "Or in it, either, to judge by the second article Carter was preparing."

Dugan looked up. "Second article? What second article?"

"The one about you giving the Slugger the office to take a dive in the big fight. He had it scheduled to run in the next issue or so."

Dugan hit the desk with his clenched fist. "That's a goddam lie!" He got up, walked to the door, let out a bellow. "Irv, get up here." Then he returned to his desk, sat drumming on the arm of his chair with stubby fingers.

Irv was Irving Salem, a former sports by-liner for the *Dispatch*, now chief of public relations for Continental. He wore a permanent frown and harried expression. He nodded to Liddell, looked to Dugan apprehensively. "Yeah, Leo?"

Dugan pointed a sausage-shaped finger at Liddell. "This peeper tells me Carter was preparing another article on the Slugger. That I had Ryan go into the tank. Check it."

"But Carter's dead, and——"

"What's the matter? I can't read the newspapers? I know goddam well he's dead. Find out about the article."

Salem bobbed his head, ran out of the office.

"I got one thing to tell you, Liddell. If that creep had run that article, I woulda saved whoever fogged him the trouble. I told him when he ran the first piece on the Slugger that no matter how many people wanted to cut his throat I'd be first on line if he ever used his name in the book again."

"And you didn't know there was going to be a second article?"

Dugan's eyes slitted, hard lumps formed on either side of his chin. "I just said so, didn't I?"

"Yeah. That's what you said, all right. And Carter's dead."

"No loss."

"The police are likely to be a little narrow-minded when a citizen stops breathing because of someone else. Even a rat like Carter. Something to do with the public health ordinance."

"You come here to tell me you're looking for the Slugger to tie in with the Carter kill. Now it's me, huh?"

Liddell shrugged. "I'm not particular. As long as I find out who it was. You'll do just as well as the Slugger."

The sausage-shaped finger jabbed at him again. "Look, peeper. Don't come around here with your funny sayings. I throw weight around in this town. Enough to separate you from that tin badge of yours." He turned irritably as Irving Salem trotted in. "Well?"

Salem licked at his lips. "I just located Hunter in a ginmill near his office. The Sportsman."

"You seem to know a lot about this mob that ran that sheet?"

Salem shook his head. "Just Hunter. We used to work on the same sheet years ago. Look, Leo——"

"Never mind the autobiography. What about the article?"

"They had one in the works. They said you knew about it, that you——"

"He's a liar," Dugan cut him off. "I'll call you if I need you." He watched the public relations man beat a nervous retreat, turned back to Liddell. "Carter's dead and the article is, too. So why don't you forget it, peeper. It'd make you a lot smarter."

"The article isn't dead, Dugan. A lot of material disappeared from Carter's place when he was killed. The only way you could be sure the article is dead is if whoever took it was going to play Santa Claus to you."

"I don't like the way that sounds."

"I don't like people who put bumps on my head, either."

"I'll tell the Slugger that."

Liddell nodded. "Do that. And tell him something else. Tell him if he's got any sense he'll look me up. I might be able to save him from getting looked up."

CHAPTER 12

The Sportsman's Bar was around the corner from 1660 Broadway, was housed in a three-story soot-stained building that was hemmed in on either side by larger, but equally nondescript structures. It was an indifferently successful attempt to reproduce an old-fashioned saloon, complete with swinging doors and sawdust on the floor.

At a quarter to six, the barroom itself was almost empty; a few regulars leaned against the bar, glasses in front of them. The bartender stood at the far end, listening with half an ear, to stories he had heard a hundred times over, polishing glasses with the other half of his consciousness. He set down a glass, balanced a half-burned cigarette on the upturned end, walked down to where Liddell took up his place.

"Ancient Age on the rocks," Liddell told him.

The man behind the stick reached for a bottle on the back shelf, brought up a glass and some ice from under the bar. He poured a scant ounce into a jigger with a phony bottom.

"Better make it a double, Jack," Liddell grunted. He watched while the bartender added another thimbleful from the jigger, pushed the glass across the bar. Liddell dropped a five alongside his glass, glanced around while the bartender was making change.

In the back of the barroom a series of booths were separated by shoulder high partitions. Bob Hunter, the editor of *Bare Facts*, was sitting in the next to last booth. He was morosely making concentric circles on the tabletop with the wet bottom of his glass.

Liddell pocketed his change, picked up his drink and walked down to where the editor sat. "Mind if I join you?"

Hunter looked up, seemed to be having difficulty focusing his eyes. "Oh, the shamus." He waved to the seat across from him grandly. "Be my guest. I'd buy you a drink, but my credit has just been shut off."

"Then you be my guest." Liddell waved down a waiter. "Give my friend a double." When the waiter hesitated, Liddell brought out a roll, separated a five from it, dropped it on the table.

The waiter shuffled toward the bar, was back in a minute with a drink. He snagged the five, made change from a pocket in his apron. When he had shuffled back out of earshot, the editor grinned at Liddell with loose lips. "Hope I didn't get you in trouble. With the cops, I mean."

"Nothing serious. What'd you tell them?"

Hunter shrugged. "Just that you were snooping around. They seemed to know you."

Liddell grinned. "I've had some dealings with them." He sipped at his drink, wondered what the Ancient Age bottle had been refilled with. "I was able to keep my skirts clean."

"Good." The editor took a deep swallow, stared blearily at Liddell over the rim of his glass. "You know they're away off. The cops, I mean."

"Why?"

"They think it was an attempted snatch or a stick-up."

"And it wasn't?"

Hunter dug a dingy handkerchief from his pocket, swabbed at his bald spot. "Hell, it could happen, I guess. Sometimes bastards like him even die in bed. But the odds are against it."

"That's what makes horse racing so interesting. Every so often the long shot wins." Liddell drained his glass, set it down. "You got any ideas you didn't give the police this morning?"

110

The editor shrugged his thin shoulders. "I gave you the list of suspects. Everyone in the telephone book. Everyone who ever knew him and a lot of people who never saw him." He tossed off his drink in a gulp. "He didn't care whose feet he stepped on."

"You knew he had a criminal record?"

Hunter puffed his lips in and out. "Wouldn't be surprised at anything."

"He had a record for extortion. Think he might have been using the magazine for blackmail?"

The editor caught the attention of the waiter, indicated the two empty glasses. When the waiter looked to Liddell for an okay, the private detective nodded.

"Hope you don't mind," Hunter grinned, "but you can't celebrate with an empty glass."

"You didn't answer my question. I asked you if you thought Carter was using the magazine for blackmail."

"You couldn't prove it by me. Wouldn't figure it from the stories he ran."

"Maybe they were the convincers. Maybe they softened up a lot of other people so he didn't have to do too much selling." He waited while the waiter replaced the two empty glasses with fresh ones, then retreated with two bills. "You said yourself he had an article set on Tony DeSales that he killed."

Hunter nodded. "That's right."

"Happen any other time?"

The editor shrugged. "I don't remember."

"I don't suppose you'd remember who sold you the article on my client?"

Hunter grinned at him, shook his head. "Never reveal a source. No good newspaperman ever does. Not even a blacklisted one like me."

"Did you buy much material from Les Ringer?"

The editor stopped with his drink halfway to his lips. "Why don't you ask Ringer?"

"I intend to."

"If your client is in the clear, why the fever?"

Liddell swirled the bourbon around the inside of his glass. "The story and the pictures have disappeared. As soon as I get them back, the fever subsides."

"That's not all that's disappeared. A half a dozen or more other articles have shown up missing."

"You have a list of them?"

"Nobody but Carter had that. I just know there were more articles on tap than the police inventory shows."

"You tell them who they were on?"

Hunter shook his head. "How could I? I just told you I'm not sure who the articles were about." He looked up at Liddell from under his lids. "The only one I could be sure about was your client. I figured I was doing her a good turn by clamming up on it."

"I'll recommend you for a Boy Scout badge," Liddell grunted. He glanced around the room, let his eyes come to rest on the editor's face. "Why do you suppose the killer took the article on my client?"

"Maybe to destroy it?"

"Now who would be that good to us?"

"You. Or even your client," Hunter told him softly.

"But there were others missing, too. You just said so."

"That's right. There were." He took a deep swallow from his glass. "That mean you're buying the police theory?"

"Which one?"

"That Carter was killed in a stick-up? That the killer took the files to set himself up in business when he couldn't find any money?"

Liddell considered it. "It might be awful risky. Whoever shows up with those files labels himself the killer."

"That is, if the ones he puts the tap on are willing to take the risk of having the stuff splashed all over the papers by fingering him."

"You know of any market for material like that?"

Hunter pursed his lips, cocked one eye. Then shook his head. "There might be a market at some of the other magazines in the field, but I don't know if they'd touch it now."

"What would you do with it if you had it?"

"That's a hypothetical question?"

Liddell nodded. "A hypothetical question."

The editor shrugged. "I think the best market for it would be the subjects themselves. Wouldn't your client have bought it back if Carter had put a price on it?"

"If the price had been only money."

Hunter shrugged. "But she was in the market to buy the stuff back? If the price was right?"

Liddell nodded. "She might still be."

"I wish I had it. The price would be right, believe me. Unfortunately, Liddell, I don't have it. And I don't know where to get it." He peered at Liddell shrewdly. "That answer the question that brought you around?"

"No. I'm not implying that you had it, Hunter. I'm just trying to figure what the next step will be of the guy who does have it." He tilted his glass to his lips, drained it. "Once I figure that out, I think I may be able to figure out how he was killed and why."

"How he was killed?"—the editor raised his

eyebrows— "There's no secret about that. He was shot through the head."

"That's what I mean. With everybody and his uncle gunning for him, how come Carter let the killer get behind him? Then again, since the gun must have been inches from Carter's head, how come there were no powder burns and how come the bullet never came through the other side?"—he grinned at the expression on the editor's face— "Like I said, finding out why he was killed was only half of it. How he was killed is even more puzzling."

"You don't think he was killed by someone trying to keep him from running a story?"

Liddell considered it, shook his head. "No, Hunter. I don't think he was killed by somebody trying to keep him from running a story. When we know why he was killed, I think we'll also know how he was killed and by whom."

Hunter watched the private detective pull himself to his feet. "I wish you'd let me know."

"I will." He glanced at his watch. "I guess I'd better be running along if I'm to catch DeSales' dinner show. What time does it break, do you know?"

Hunter shrugged, consulted his watch. "It's after six now. He comes offstage about seven or seven-thirty, I'd guess."—he squinted up at Liddell curiously— "You going to see him about the article?"

"That and a couple of other things."

"Such as?"

"Such as whether or not Les Ringer could have sold Carter the material about him. And how he kept it from being printed. It might come in handy for my client in case the material shows up again."

"Why Les Ringer?"

"I'm going to have a little session with Les tonight and I'd like to go in loaded. I've got a feeling he might know more about what's going on than he realizes."

CHAPTER 13

The Criterion Theatre on the corner of 44th Street and Broadway was Mecca for the blue jeans and bubble gum set this week. In electric letters, five feet high, it bragged about the booking of Tony DeSales for a "limited in-person appearance."

On Broadway, the street was clogged with a squirming mass of teen-agers in a queue that led to the box office, pushing and shoving in their eagerness to get in. Inside, the seats were occupied by the same patrons who had shown up for the first show, had taken title to a seat and spent their time between stage shows in the lounge, primping and squealing.

At the side of the Criterion lobby there was a twelve foot cutout of DeSales, revealing him to be a slack-lipped, liquid-eyed man in a dark sports jacket and matching slacks. His hair was thick and oily,

117

pasted close to his head above the ears, fluffed into carefully contrived casual curls on top.

An usher was assigned to come out every hour with a wet brush to wipe the lipstick smears from the cutout's hands. One enterprising fan had even persuaded her escort to let her stand on his shoulders while she pressed her smeary mouth against the reproduction of DeSales' lips to the accompaniment of cheers from the crowd.

The management pretended to frown on the adulation, was secretly considering adding another life-sized portrait of the crooner for the possible publicity value.

Johnny Liddell shouldered his way through the crowd out front, headed for the 44th Street stage door. Here again there was a mass of screaming, wild-eyed fans resisting all efforts of the police to keep the stage door clear. Liddell located a policeman he knew, prevailed upon him to open a path through the crowd. Inside the stage door, the cop took his uniform hat from his head, wiped his forehead on his sleeve.

"I'd rather buck a mob of striking longshoremen," he grunted. He held up his hand, showed Liddell the marks of a set of teeth that had broken the skin. "They kick and bite and claw and everything else. I never saw anything like it. Not even with Sinatra or Presley, and God knows that was rough

118

enough." He replaced his hat, grinned. "Didn't figure you for a DeSales fan, though."

"Fan, hell. I'd rather kick him right in the middle of his guitar from what I've seen so far. I've got to talk to the creep, but I'm not looking forward to it."

"You're not looking forward to it. I got a deal for you. I'll talk to him, you reason with that mob out there."

Liddell grinned at him. "Thank you very much, but no thanks." He waited until the policeman had opened the door wide enough to slip out, then headed down the corridor toward the entrance to the dressing rooms.

An old man sat at the door, his chair tilted back against the wall, a short-stemmed briar gripped between his teeth, reading *Variety*. He looked up as Liddell approached, peered at him nearsightedly, then grinned when he recognized the private detective.

"Hello, Johnny." He let the front legs of the chair hit the floor, pulled the pipe from between his teeth. "Wasn't figuring to be seeing you back here this week." He knocked the dottle from the pipe, brought a worn leather pouch from his pocket. "Who you want to see?"

"DeSales."

The old man frowned, dug the bowl of the pipe

into the pouch, started packing it with his index finger. "They expecting you back there?"

"They?"

"Him and that secretary of his. She's supposed to give me an okay for everybody who gets back to see him." He stuck the pipe between his teeth, rattled the juice in the stem. "Guess it's okay, though, if you're doing a job for him."

"From what I hear, I'd rather be doing a job on him. What kind of a guy is he?"

The old man scratched a wooden match along the wall, held it to the bowl of the pipe. "A conceited little bastard," he grunted without rancor. "We've had all kinds back here in the ten years I been on the door. This one is the daddy of them all."

"He still onstage?"

The doorman consulted an old pocket watch, nodded. "The girl's back there, though. One that calls herself his secretary."

"Is she?"

"Could be, I suppose. Looks like she has too much sense to go for a freak like him, but you can never tell. Know where it is?"

Liddell shook his head.

"Dressing Room B. Third on the left. He should be off in a couple of minutes." He watched Liddell head toward the dressing rooms beyond, went back to his copy of *Variety*.

120

From the wings came the muted sound of a band with a big beat, the stamping of hundreds of feet. Liddell stopped for a moment to listen, shook his head, knocked at the door to Dressing Room B.

The girl who opened the door wore a tight-fitting sweater, a sheathlike skirt. Neither did her a disservice. Her dark hair was clipped short, curled around her face. Her eyes were a startling blue, faintly shadowed; her full lips had a petulant droop.

"My name is Liddell. I'm supposed to have a talk with DeSales."

"Are you expected?"

"I might be. By now he's heard about Murray Carter being killed." He caught the faint flicker of the girl's eyes. "I'm trying to keep him out of the investigation."

"He's onstage."

Liddell nodded. "I'll wait."

The dark-haired girl nodded, stood aside as he walked in. Her eyes took in the set of his shoulders, the heavy jaw, the thick hair spiked with grey. She seemed to approve. "Glad to have some company."

The dressing room was larger than average, had in addition to the usual dressing table and chair a sagging leather couch and two wardrobe closets. The girl walked over to the couch, dropped onto it, drew her legs up under her. She watched with serious eyes while Liddell swung the wooden chair around, straddled it.

"Is there going to be trouble?"

Liddell shrugged. "Part of my job is to avoid it. There haven't been any reporters yet?"

The girl shook her head. "You know the way he is. He probably wouldn't talk to them anyhow. He thinks they're trying to tear him down."

"I don't know how he is. How is he?"

"Cornball. But he sends those kids. You have any trouble getting through the mob at the stage door?"

"I used a flying wedge of cops. Is it always like that?"

"Always. That's why I don't leave even between shows. Every time I see that mob closing in on us, I get claustrophobia."

"When they stop doing it, he's dead."

"I suppose so. But they sure don't show any signs of stopping. It gets worse every place we work."

Liddell grunted. "What do you figure makes the kids go for him the way they do?"

"Because they're kids, I guess. They latch onto an offbeat character like DeSales because he kicks over all the rules and gets away with it. He gets rich doing the things they dream about doing but don't have the nerve to try."

"And you?"

"What about me?"

"What do you think about him?"

"You kidding?" The girl picked a cigarette from the pack on the arm of the couch, tapped it. "I work for the character. If you have me pegged as part of a private harem, forget it."

"That's his tough luck."

The girl stuck the cigarette in the corner of her mouth, smiled. "Thanks, but he wouldn't think so. I'm an old hag in his book. He likes them young. Real young."

Liddell scratched a match, held it out to her. "Look, I can't just call you Hey You. Got a name?" He blew out the match, tossed it at an ash tray on the dressing table. "Mine's Johnny. Johnny Liddell."

"Betty Marks." She took a deep drag, blew the smoke at the ceiling. "I suppose you're wondering what part I play in this menagerie?"

"It had crossed my mind."

"I'm his keeper. And believe me, with a young bull like this who doesn't like a ring in his nose, it's not easy."

"A problem, eh?"

"Problem? You mean problems. It's never the same kid twice, and all jailbait. Trying to reason with this character is like trying to talk to a stone wall— and you'd probably get more sensible answers. The only way you can throw a scare into this guy is to tell him one of these chippies is going to lasso him and shotgun him into making her an honest woman."

Liddell grinned. "He doesn't believe in matrimony, I take it?"

"He thinks it's strictly for the birds. One of his favorite sayings is why buy a cow when you can get milk through the fence."

"A real philosopher."

The girl cocked her head toward the door. "He's finishing up now. He'll be back in a couple of minutes."

Liddell got up from the chair, walked to the door, opened it. From the wings came a deep-throated roar that rose to a peak of screaming voices, high-pitched whistles underscored by the stamping of feet.

"This is something you should see once. Just once," the girl told him. "He's in the wings now, watching them squirm and squeal and getting a big boot out of it. He'll tease them for a moment, then shuffle out for another bow. Listen."

Almost as though on cue, the wave of noise seemed to recede for a second, then it roared back with renewed force.

"By now, the girls are dancing in the aisles, fighting the special cops to get close enough to touch him. It happens every place he works and he loves it."

"He sounds like a real ripe character." Liddell closed the door, cutting off the noise.

124

"Real ripe."

There was a brief pause, then the door to the dressing room burst open, was slammed shut. Tony DeSales was dressed in the same colored jacket and slacks as in the cutout in the lobby. The curls on top were slightly disarrayed, but the lacquered sides were stiffly in place. His mouth was a wet smear.

"Creamed them." He winked at the girl. "You hear them out there screaming for more? That's the way I leave them, screaming for more."

"So I notice." The girl nodded to Liddell. "Here's someone from the boss. To talk to you about that publisher who was murdered."

DeSales seemed to notice Liddell for the first time. "You from Minelli?"

"No. I'm a private detective working on the Carter kill."

The girl stopped the cigarette halfway to her lips. "But I took for granted you were working for Minelli, keeping Tony out of it."

"You assume too much," the crooner spat at her. He turned back to Liddell. "You better blow, mister. I don't like cops, brass buttons or private. Out."

"After I get what I came for. The answer to a couple of questions."

DeSales sneered at him, deliberately turned his

back, checked his appearance in the mirror. Liddell caught him by the arm, spun him around.

"Now, wait a minute, Liddell—" the girl got up from the couch, caught Liddell's arm.

"Stay out of this." DeSales put his hand on the girl's chest, sent her reeling backwards toward the couch. "You're to blame for letting him in and you don't get off the hook that easy." He turned back to Liddell. "And you, crumb. You put your hand on me again and I'll cut it off."

Liddell caught him by the lapel of his jacket, pulled the crooner toward him. DeSales' hand streaked for his pocket, came out with a knife. He snapped open the blade, touched the point against Liddell's throat.

"Get your hand off me." His voice was low, hard.

Liddell released the lapel.

"I ought to carve my initials in your neck for that." He pricked the skin on the detective's neck with the point of the blade. "That's just a souvenir."

Liddell touched his finger to the nick on his neck, brought away a minute drop of blood. He stared at it bleakly for a minute, then wiped it on the palm of his hand. DeSales watched him with a sneering grin, the knife held at ready. The girl sat on the couch, chewing on her lower lip.

Suddenly, Liddell lashed out with his heel, caught the crooner on the shin. DeSales yelped,

126

dropped the knife. He clasped his shin with both hands, hopped around, screaming his rage.

"Get somebody in here. Get that bum out of here before I kill him," he screamed at the girl.

"You told me to stay out of it," she told him.

DeSales started for the door, didn't make it. Liddell yanked him back off balance and when the crooner opened his mouth to yell, he slashed him across the Adam's apple with the side of his hand. DeSales' face turned purple, he gagged.

"I'm getting pretty tired of letting crumbs like you get the idea they can tee off on me."

DeSales tried to knee him, Liddell slammed him across the face with the flat of his hand, sent him staggering back to crash into the wall. DeSales slid to the floor, whimpering.

"Minelli isn't going to like this, Liddell," the girl told him. "He's not going to like it even a little bit." She made no move to get help.

"I came for some answers and I don't care how stubborn he gets. The longer it takes me to get the answers out of him, the better I'm going to like it." He walked over to where DeSales sat, massaging his throat.

Liddell caught him by the hair, pulled him to his feet and pushed him into the chair.

DeSales was no longer dapper. The carefully shellacked hair hung dankly in his face; the large liquid eyes were watery; the purple lips were blue. He was having trouble breathing.

"You had a beef with Murray Carter. About an article he was going to run."

The man in the chair managed to croak, "No article on me ran in his rag."

"That's just the point. Why didn't it run?"

DeSales glared at him, refused to open his mouth.

"Going to get stubborn?" Liddell picked up the crooner's knife, tested the point on the ball of his thumb. "Wonder how many of those chippies will like your new face?"

DeSales looked from the knife to Liddell and back. Perspiration glistened along his hair line. "You're not scaring me."

The girl on the couch laughed softly. "You could fool me. From here it looks like you're shaking yourself loose from your porcelain jackets."

The crooner cast her a baleful glare, started to retort. Liddell cut him off by sinking his fingers into DeSales' thick hair, pulling his head back until his eyes watered. "How did you keep the article from running?" Liddell stared down into his face. "You pay off?"

"No."

Liddell touched the point of the knife to the

crooner's face. DeSales flinched, the color drained from his face.

"What did you do? Set up some of the others for a frame so he could do articles on them?"

"What do you think I am? A rat?"

Liddell grinned bleakly. "Don't ask leading questions, buster. If you didn't pay off and you didn't work with him, why should he lay off you?"

DeSales set his lips stubbornly. Liddell yanked on the hair, drew a wince.

"Why?"

"Minelli made him lay off."

Liddell released the crooner's hair. "How come Minelli let him do the article in the first place if—" He broke off. "Minelli wasn't your manager when Carter was bugging you, was he?"

DeSales's eyes darted around the room. When Liddell made a motion toward him, he cowered back. "No. That's why I signed with Minelli. To get Carter off my back."

Liddell snapped his fingers. "So that's it. So that's the gimmick. Carter puts on the heat, Minelli moves in and promises to get the heat off if you sign up with him."

"So?"

Liddell tossed the knife on the dressing table. "Real smart. On a straight shakedown the best they could come up with is five, ten thousand. But on a management contract on a hot property they could net ten times that."

DeSales looked stricken. "Look, you didn't get that from me, mister. I'm no stool."

"Like the lady says, you could fool me." He walked to the door. "If I were you, I wouldn't mention my little visit to Minelli right now. When he finds out what I'm thinking he might get the idea you are a stool."

CHAPTER 14

Pinky had left
by the time Johnny Liddell returned to the office. As he put his key into the lock, the phone started shrilling. He shoved open the door, sprinted to her desk, lifted the receiver to his ear.

"Yeah?"

The voice on the other end was low, guarded. "That you, shamus?"

"Who's this?"

"Les Ringer." There was a slight pause, Liddell could hear the man's heavy breathing. "That client of yours could be in a bad spot if I wanted to get nasty. You know what I mean?"

"You tell me."

"With Carter getting himself dead just a few hours after you rough up a guy because he sold Carter some stuff on her, the papers could have a real picnic with it. That get to you?"

"My client's in the clear."

"Sure, but what's that got to do with it? Her name in the headlines and a lot of teat art could sell an awful lot of papers."

"There's nothing to tie my client to Carter."

Ringer laughed softly. "Just because the article didn't show up when the cops shook the place down. Maybe it could still show up."

Liddell considered. "This is no way to talk it over. Why don't you drop by here?"

"No can do, shamus. I might have a couple of other people I want to talk it over with first." Liddell could picture the bubbles forming and breaking in the center of the man's pouty lips. "But I'm not dealing you out. I usually get paid for getting things into the papers. In your case I might make an exception and get paid for keeping them out."

"Let's talk about it."

"Okay. But if the hands get in the way like they did last time, what I got goes to the papers no matter what happens to me."

"Where and when?"

There was a pause. "You know the Miss America Ballroom on Forty-fourth?"

"The dime a dance joint?"

"Yeah. I'm press agenting the place. I make it every night about twelve to hold the boss's hand. I'll be there tonight."

Liddell started to argue, heard the click as the phone on the other end was hung up. The line went dead. He dropped his receiver on its hook, walked into his office.

A note speared on the spindle informed him that Red Daniels would wait for a call from him at Acme until nine, then could be reached at home. He poured himself a stiff shot of bourbon from the bottle in the bottom drawer. It was a few minutes after eight when he reached Red Daniels. The redhead promised to come right up.

Liddell was standing at the window, staring down at the lengthening shadows in the park across the street when Red Daniels walked in. He carried a manila envelope, which he dropped on the corner of the desk.

"How'd it go?" Liddell wanted to know.

"All right. I've been able to check all of them." He indicated the bottle on the desk. "Just for ornamental purposes?"

Liddell dropped into the chair. "Help yourself." He waited while Daniels poured himself a shot, tossed it off. "Any possibles?"

Daniels settled his lanky frame in the customer's chair, reached for the envelope and dumped out a few sheets of paper. "Only a few were in town last night as far as I could check."

133

Liddell pulled over a yellow pad, picked up a pencil. "Let's have them."

The redhead consulted his notes. "You can scratch Laurie Evans. She's singing with Del Cort's band, you know." Liddell nodded. "They're doing a series of one nighters. They were at the Starlight Gardens in St. Louis last night."

Liddell nodded, ran a line through the girl's name. "Who else?"

"Sonny Morris, the hood. He owns a piece of a joint in Vegas. He's been out there all week meeting with his partners." He ran his eye over a few typewritten lines on the report. "I had our boy out there check on the possibility that he could have hopped a plane and popped back into town and right out."

Liddell looked up. "And?"

"No soap. Sonny got on the dice at the Last Chance around midnight last night, got hot and was still rolling them this morning according to our boy."

Liddell scratched the name off the list. "How about Leo Dugan?"

"In town. So was Slugger Ryan."

Liddell touched the tender spot on the side of his jaw. "I know all about the Slugger," he grunted. He circled the name of Leo Dugan on the pad. "So Leo was available last night too, huh?" He ran the pencil around the name of Tony DeSales. "We know

DeSales was. He's doing a personal appearance at the Criterion." He made dots alongside the remaining three names. "How about the others—Marissoff, Tim Carpenter and Mike Regan."

"Carpenter is supposed to be off on a cruise someplace."

"Supposed to be?"

"Well, he hasn't been seen in any of his favorite haunts for the past few weeks. He was in Palm Beach a month ago sponging off some wealthy friends, so chances are he did latch onto a free boatride."

Liddell ran a tentative line through Carpenter's name. "Marissoff?"

"In town." He looked up from his notes. "A pretty gamy character, I gather. Travels with a real weird crowd."

"Plenty gamy. That Cafe Society kick she's on hardly ever leaves them smelling like violets." He circled her name. "Mike Regan?"

"At the Ambassador. He's in for the opening of his new picture." He folded the papers, stowed them in the manila envelope. "He went out on the town last night, hasn't shown back at the hotel yet. Whisper is that he ended up in Harlem and is still padded down up there."

Liddell traced a question mark after the actor's name. "He apparently has a real yen for dark meat.

135

He must have known Carter was going to run that piece on his Harlem binges but he still can't stay away."

"Carter sure had these characters taped wherever he got his information."

"Hell, my files and your files could keep a rag like that going for years if we put them up for sale. And there are some shady ops who do put a price on their files."

"I can buy that on divorce stuff and background material, but how many ops have stuff like the Regan material in their files?"

"The town is crawling with fringe characters who are tickled to death to dig the stuff for guys like Carter. There's no secret about Regan and his uptown yen in his circles. Some borderline press agent or even some guy working for Regan's company turns a fast buck by writing it up."

"You think a story like that would burn Regan enough to make him kill? Like you say, he doesn't try to cover it up."

"It might. It could ruin him down South. A boycott on his pictures down there could put him out of business. He might get desperate enough. Especially if he had been blowing tea."

"How many possibles have you got?"

"Five who had both the motive and the opportunity." He sucked his lips in, blew them out thoughtfully. "There are a couple of others like my client and Sal Minelli who weren't on that list I gave you. If you add them and one of Carter's sources I'm checking out tonight and the guy that worked for Carter you've got nine live possibles."

"How do you figure to check them out?"

Liddell grinned. "I intend to ask them." He consulted his wrist watch. "I've got a date at midnight. Think you can get me a line on where Mike Regan is likely to be holed up in Harlem?"

"It's probably an after hours joint. The place is loaded with them."

"Shake them down for me, will you, Red? If you get a line on it, call it in to my answering service. I'll check her at about twelve."

Daniels pulled himself out of his chair. "I'll make a real college try." He reached for the bourbon bottle, spilled some into the glass. "One for the road." He tossed the drink off, made a face. "Damned if I know why I drink the stuff. I hate the taste of it."

Liddell waited until he heard the redhead close the door to the corridor behind him. Then he loosened his tie, leaned back in his chair and hooked his heels on the corner of his desk. He was asleep in five minutes.

The Miss America Ballroom is on the north-west corner of 44th Street and Broadway. A string of blinking, multicolored lights throws interesting shadows on the flyspecked studio photographs of tired-looking blondes and brunettes in a dust-covered showcase at the street level.

The flat, nasal tones of a barker spill out onto the street to clash with the traffic sounds. "Come and see 'em, boys! Fifty of 'em. Fifty of the most gorgeous show girls on Broadway waiting to dance with you. Come in and meet 'em!"

Johnny Liddell dropped the cab on the corner, turned and checked his watch with the big Paramount clock. It was almost 12:20.

He walked down the flight of steps to the ballroom, stopped in front of the ticket booth. A fat disheveled blonde sat behind the glass of the booth, chewed her wad of gum with the contentment of a cow chewing its cud. She pushed a strip of tickets through the aperture, scooped up Liddell's dollar bill, regarded him with blank, unseeing eyes. He pushed his way through the turnstile under the unfriendly eye of a huge ticket taker dressed to resemble an admiral, passed into the ballroom itself.

It was a huge, upholstered cellar lit with dim blue lights. The air was heavily spiced with an odor compounded of equal parts of perspiration and cheap perfume. A multicolored globe in the ceiling revolved over the floor, shooting spangles of light at the floor.

138

There, slowly gyrating couples were locked in close embraces, the hostesses making circular rhythmic motions with their hips, the customers trying desperately to get everything to which their ticket entitled them.

Liddell found himself a place at the railing that ringed the dance floor, looked around. Off to the left, a group of hostesses clustered together, laughing, chattering, bickering. One of them, a heavy-set blonde, peeled off from the group, paraded in front of Liddell with an exaggerated flip of her hips, dancing solo in time to the music and finishing off with a quick bump.

"Like to dance?" Her voice was heavy, raspy. In the half light, her lips were heavily rouged, her eyes heavy lidded. Her gown was cut in a deep V that bared the deep cleft between her breasts. She reeked of cheap perfume.

"Not right now. I'm looking for Les Ringer."

The blonde sniffed. "That phony. He's all the time setting us up for some publicity, but all he ever does is set us up. I'd be more fun," she rasped.

"It shouldn't take long."

She shrugged. "He uses the rear storeroom for an office. I don't know if he's in. I didn't see him tonight."

Liddell nodded. He walked to the rear, skirted a row of rickety wooden tables where couples and stags were drinking beer from paper cups. The light was dimmer back here, no one paid him any attention as he headed toward the rear storeroom.

The door was closed, but a thin ribbon of light was visible under it. Liddell rapped his knuckles against it, decided that a knock couldn't be heard above the racket of the five piece combo. He tried the knob, found it open and pushed the door open.

Ringer's "office" was a windowless cubbyhole just barely big enough for a desk and chair. The air in the room was close, foul.

Les Ringer sat in a chair behind the desk, his head resting on the back of it. His normally ruddy face was grey, his wide eyes were fixed with horrible intensity on the doorway in which Liddell stood. A thin trickle of blood ran from the corner of his mouth, coursed down the side of his chin. It matched in color the dark stain on the front of his shirt.

Liddell cursed softly, stepped in, closed the door behind him. He circled the desk, touched the dead man's hand. It was already beginning to grow cold. Quickly, Liddell took the desk drawers one by one, riffled through their contents, found nothing of interest. In the breast of the man's pocket he found several envelopes containing rejects from columnists, a sheaf of papers with scribbled gossip notations. None seemed to have any bearing on why he was killed.

Liddell returned to the door, switched off the light in the room. He opened the door a crack, put his eye to it. When he was sure no one was paying his end of the room any attention, he slid out and closed the door after him.

He had no doubt that the key to Ringer's death lay in some knowledge he had of Carter's killing. It wasn't in the "office" and the risk of possible discovery while checking his room at the hotel was too great in the light of the possible momentary discovery of the body. If he could delay the entry of the police into Ringer's murder for a few hours. . . .

He decided to take a gamble.

At the bank of telephone booths, he consulted the Manhattan directory, got the number of the Miss America Ballroom. He stepped into a booth from which he could see the broad back of the ticket taker at the turnstile. He dialed the number, waited.

Finally, a woman's voice rasped. "Miss America Ballroom."

"You better get to the rear storeroom. There's a dead man in there."

He could hear the gasp at the other end as he hung up. Quickly, he stepped out of the booth, mixed with the other patrons at the rail. He caught the eye of a hostess, signaled her over.

In the dim light she didn't look to be over twenty. Her hair was thick, cascaded down over her shoulders. Her midriff was bare, she wore a halter top to her black gown that eliminated any possibility that she wore anything under it. Her lips were full, soft-looking.

"Want to dance?" she invited.

Liddell pushed his strip of tickets into her hand. She folded them, dropped them into her purse. She waited until Liddell came out onto the floor, melted against him.

He could see plenty of activity near the turnstile. Two men in tuxedoes pushed their way past the ticket taker, headed toward the rear. The oversized ticket taker stared after them open mouthed.

Liddell was aware of the body of the girl glued against him as she started to undulate slowly, insinuatingly. They barely moved from the one spot; every ounce of the girl's 118 pounds seemed to be in motion except for her feet.

The band raced through a chorus, then the lights came up.

From the rear of the building, one of the tuxedoed guards came at a near trot. He stopped long enough to whisper something to the ticket taker, then rushed out.

The music started up again, the girl slid into Liddell's arms.

"Haven't seen you here before." She leaned her

head against his shoulder, hummed softly in time to the music. "You're not the usual type."

"What is the type?"

"Fat slobs with two left feet and more hands than an octopus."

As the music stepped up in tempo, she started to undulate again. Liddell was having increasing difficulty in concentrating his attention on the passage to the rear office. Finally, when the lights came up again, he caught the girl by the arm, led her back toward the railing.

"You still have two more dances," she pouted. "Didn't you like?"

Liddell grinned at her. "I liked real fine, but I'd have to go into training to last through two more like that and still walk away."

A fat, sweat-flecked man pushed his way through the crowd at the railing, caught the girl and whirled her toward the center of the floor as Liddell released her. Liddell headed for a table, ordered a paper cup of beer, sipped it slowly.

From where he sat, he could see one of the tuxedoed guards leaning against the wall in the corridor leading to Ringer's office, working on his nails with a small pocketknife. There was no sign of the other man. The detective took his time about finishing his beer, then he got up and headed for the turnstile and the street.

Liddell wasn't too sure of what would happen in the Miss America Ballroom in the next few hours. The only thing he was sure of was that no police would be called to the ballroom and that Ringer's body, when it turned up, would be far from the Miss America Ballroom.

CHAPTER 15

Johnny Liddell
ambled nonchalantly into the lobby of the Hotel William, nodded briefly to the man behind the registration desk, drew an uncertain nod in return. The man who had been on duty the night before when he and Les Ringer had gone to the press agent's room was apparently off duty after midnight, replaced by a younger, but equally watery-eyed version.

Liddell crossed the lobby as though he had lived there for years, picked up a *Daily News* from the folding chair next to the elevator, and dropped a dime in the topless cigar box.

The elevator operator pulled his attention away from a tattered paperback edition of Richard Prather's *Find This Woman* with obvious reluctance. Liddell had already retreated behind the opened pages of his newspaper.

"Four."

The elevator operator slammed the cage door shut, coaxed it into jerky motion. It shuddered to a stop at the fourth floor. He barely wasted a glance in Liddell's direction as the detective headed down the hall in the direction of Ringer's room. When the groans of the descending cage were barely audible, Liddell stopped in front of 408, tried the knob, found it locked.

He brought the thin strip of celluloid from his pocket, used it on the door with success. There was a faint click, the knob turned in his hand. He pushed the door open, stepped into the room and closed the door behind him.

The bridge lamp still spilled its yellow puddle of light onto the worn carpet. The grey-white linen on the bed was in what was apparently its customary state of disarray; opened pages of the *Journal-American* were strewn around the room. A soiled shirt for which Les Ringer would never again have earthly use was draped over the back of the chair.

Johnny Liddell stood for a moment, looked around the room. There seemed to be very little doubt that Ringer had something more than conversation which he intended to sell to the highest bidder. The question was where would a man like Ringer hide the material that bought him a slug in the chest for his trouble?

146

Liddell's eyes hopscotched around the room, decided that the rickety, paint-peeled dresser was the logical place to begin. When he yanked open the first drawer it was apparent that he wasn't the only one who had reached the conclusion that Ringer had something of value hidden. Drawer after drawer showed the effects of a careful ransacking. They yielded nothing of interest.

Next came the bed, then the top of the closet, under the rug.

Liddell was almost ready to admit defeat when, as a matter of routine, he examined the sink in the bathroom. Attached to the underside by strips of adhesive tape was a small leather-covered memo book. He took it out, examined it under the light of the bridge lamp. The front part of the book was devoted to notes, names, dates and places concerning well-known names. The last few pages had been used as a ledger.

Each week, Ringer carefully noted his income on one page and his expenses on another. Some weeks he went into the red, others he ended up with a profit. There were four sales to *Bare Facts* listed in the ledger section. The press agent had gotten $200 each for articles on Celeste Pierce, Tony DeSales, Mike Regan and Slugger Ryan.

Liddell turned to the front of the book, glanced

through the notes on Celeste Pierce. There was a date at the end of the article, apparently the expected publication date.

A similar date had been penciled on the last page of the notes on Tony DeSales, then crossed out and a question mark put in its place. Another question mark followed Mike Regan's name, but Slugger Ryan's name had a heavy check and a circled date next to it. Apparently, only one of Les Ringer's articles had appeared on schedule.

Liddell dropped the memo book into his side jacket pocket. He took a last look around the little room. It was obvious that Les Ringer had kept no copies of the articles he had done on the four or that if he had they were no longer in the room.

He was about to leave when the knob to the door turned slowly, softly. Quickly, Johnny Liddell doused the light, stepped back behind the door.

There was a moment's pause, then the knob turned again. This time he could hear the sound of a key scraping into the lock. He flattened himself against the wall, slipped the .45 from its hammock into his right hand.

The key turned in the lock, the door started to inch open. A yellow stain of light spilled into the room from the corridor, reached for the unmade bed.

Liddell held his breath as the snout of a .38 special shoved into the room, was followed by the burly figure of a man. As soon as the man was into the room, Liddell swung. The barrel of the .45 caught the newcomer above the ear, knocked him to his knees. He struggled to bring the .38 to firing position. A second blow flattened him out on his face.

Liddell caught him under the arms, dragged him into the room, closed the door behind him. Then, he turned on the bridge lamp, studied the unconscious man. He was heavy in the shoulder, wore a stained grey fedora which, at the moment, was badly dented.

Liddell turned him over on his back, failed to recognize the battered features of the unconscious man. He dug his hand into the breast pocket of his jacket, came up with a well-worn wallet. He flipped through the cards and identification in the wallet, groaned.

The unconscious man was William V. Moloney, security officer for the Hotel William.

Hastily, he replaced the wallet in the man's pocket, walked to the door, opened it a crack. When he was satisfied the corridor was empty, he stepped out, closed the door behind him. He walked to the red light indicating the staircase, walked down to the second floor. There, he leaned on the button for the elevator until he heard the slam of the closing doors below. When the cage started to whine its way upward, he walked down the steps to the lobby.

The man behind the desk was engrossed in biting the cuticle on his left thumb, didn't bother to look up as the private detective unhurriedly crossed the lobby.

As Liddell reached the door, he could hear the insistent buzzing of the switchboard. The clerk took his time about answering it. Somebody on the fourth floor was in an awful hurry to reach the desk. By the time they did, Liddell had already melted into the crowds still thronging Broadway.

At the all-night drugstore on the corner of 47th and Broadway, he stepped into a booth and phoned his answering service. Red Daniels had left a number with a request for Liddell to call him regardless of the hour.

He dialed the number the service had given him, lighted a cigarette while he waited, stared out into the neon drenched streets beyond. After a moment, the sleepy voice of Red Daniels came on.

"Sorry to be so late getting back to you, Red," Liddell told him. "I've been up to my neck. Get anything for me?"

The redhead suppressed a yawn. "Maybe. Maybe not. You ever hear of a place called Matty Lou's in Harlem?"

Liddell considered, shook his head. "I haven't been in Harlem in years. What about it?"

"I haven't got anything definite. Just rumors. But this joint is supposed to be the big thing up there. It's an after hours joint where you can get anything. The downtown crowd gives it a big play after the Stem joints close."

"Regan?"

"He's made the joint from what I gather. Has a chick on the staff up there. Anyway, that's the whisper."

"How do I make the connect?"

Daniels was silent for a moment. "That's the bug, Johnny. You've got to be a member. They got a good thing going for them and they don't take too many chances."

"But?"

"You say you haven't worked Harlem in a couple of years. You likely to get made by any of the regulars?"

"I don't think so."

"Word is she does use some steerers. Maybe you could make a connect with one of them and get okayed in. If you looked like ready money set up for a quick take, some of the larceny in the gal shows through."

"Any ideas?"

"I don't know Harlem too well myself," the redhead conceded, "but I do know one after hours joint that runs pretty wide open. Maybe you could make the connect there."

"It's worth a try. Got an address on it?"

"Fats Riva runs it. He's an old-time pug run to fat. It's a peephole setup and the only introduction you need is a folded bill. You get the okay from a lookout in front of the joint. That's at 118th and Park."

Liddell nodded. "Thanks."

"Johnny, be careful. Those boys up there are liable to be a little excitable."

"Yeah." Liddell dropped the receiver on the hook, pushed open the door to the booth. He dug Les Ringer's memo book from his pocket, checked through the notes on Mike Regan. The initials M.L. could mean Matty Lou. He put the book away, decided things were beginning to look up.

He did something he hadn't done in years. He slid onto a stool at the counter and ordered an ice cream soda.

CHAPTER 16

At two o'clock
in the morning, the streets in Harlem are little different from the streets at two o'clock in the afternoon. The pedestrian must run the gantlet between the stoop sitters and the other refugees from steaming apartments who perch on wooden boxes that line the curb.

On the sidewalk, men and women shuffle by in a seemingly never-ending stream—the men zoot-suited, colorful peacocks; the women drab, prematurely aged, tired. The slowly moving tide of white, black, yellow and brown continues to ebb and flow along the street tirelessly.

Johnny Liddell dropped the cab at 116th and Park, walked north toward 118th. A dusky-faced girl in a tight fitting blouse sidled up to him. She was small, thin, high breasted. Her mouth was a bright red smear, her teeth uneven, bad.

"You like girl?" she whispered with a soft Latin accent. "You come with Chica, Chu-Chi. Chica much fun." She rolled her eyes lewdly.

Liddell started to brush by her.

"Oy, wassa matta, Chu-Chi? You no like Chica? Chica much good. I much fun."

Liddell grinned at her. "I'll bet. Some other time."

The girl watched him stride past, flung up her skirt, wiggled her hips at him obscenely. "*Maricón*," she screamed after him.

As he walked along Park Avenue, Liddell marveled at the change a few blocks make in an avenue. Less than a mile behind, huge apartment buildings housed expensive apartments, mink-coated women, tuxedoed men. There, sleek Cadillacs and Jags purred along, trying to make the lights.

Up here, a *bodega* spilt raucous Spanish music into the street. The usual high-pitched chatter hit a new high with *cervesa* and *ron* brought home with the paychecks. Somebody close by was laughing shrilly, someplace else someone would be crying. They'd be making love, beating their wives, drinking themselves into insensibility. Large numbers of people were crowded into one room, living and eating and reproducing within arm's reach of each other. And dying, too, probably.

This was Spanish Harlem where the people were

like a calendar, disappearing from the streets to huddle around oil heaters in their flats in the late fall; emerging pale and wan in the spring; crowding the sidewalks with chattering, laughing confusion in the summer.

This was the area which, in Liddell's youth, had been almost exclusively Irish and the Irish had ruled it with an iron hand. When the Jews and Italians started to invade this Irish stronghold, they were met with flying fists and brickbats. But as more and more came, the strength of the Irish waned and they, in turn, retreated before the greater numbers, the beatings, the flying bottles.

Then came the Negro to challenge the control of the Italians. Race wars ranged from 96th Street where the New York Central pokes its tracks up through the carefully terraced width of Park Avenue to climb aboard its uptown trestle up to 125th Street. Slowly, inexorably and by sheer force of numbers, the Negroes pushed the Italians out.

But even then the fight for possession wasn't over. Planeload after planeload brought thin, underfed and underclothed natives from San Juan and Mayagüez and the rest of Puerto Rico to find the gold that Vito Marcantonio and his political henchmen assured them lay in the streets and gutters of New York. In the face of this invasion, the Negro retreated farther and farther north, practically disappeared from the 96th Street area, resettled north of 125th Street.

On the corner of 118th, a group of teen-agers clustered around the newsstand in front of a candy store. From inside came the wail of a jukebox.

Johnny Liddell walked in, bought a pack of Chesterfields, tore open the package. The man behind the counter watched him with unfriendly eyes. He hung a cigarette in the corner of his mouth, touched a match to it.

"Where could a stranger in town get a little action?" he asked the man behind the counter.

The man shrugged, shook his head.

"Heard a man could get some action up here if he knew the right people." He dipped his hand into his pocket, brought up a folded five. He held it so the numeral would show. "Got any ideas?"

The man behind the counter stared at the five reflectively. "A man might be able to get himself a drink." His eyes rolled up to Liddell's face. "Some girls around. Might be able to get you one."

Liddell blew a stream of smoke at the ceiling. "Let's start with the drink. All the places I know are closed." He reached over the counter, the five changed hands.

The counterman ambled to the door, looked up and down the street in both directions. Then he nodded for Liddell to follow him to the rear of the store. An "Out of Order" sign hung askew on one of the booths. He entered it, slid back the rear partition.

The room beyond was a big, barnlike place. Three couples were dancing to the music from a jukebox; the women might as well have worn tags identifying their profession. Each in turn gave Liddell a calculating glance as he walked in. Several more women were wedged in with the men at the bar. Lining the walls were spindly-looking tables, all filled. Most of the men in the place were drinking beer out of cans, there was a lot of swearing, mauling going on at the tables.

The reason for the blaring jukebox in the store beyond was immediately apparent.

Liddell found himself a place at the bar, pointed to a bottle of Grand Dad on the back bar. "Let's have a double shot." While the bartender was pouring the shot, Liddell turned his back to the bar, looked around. Some of the patrons at the far tables were getting sloppy drunk. A short hulking bouncer leaned against the wall left of the partition through which Liddell had entered. He was twirling a toy baseball bat, watching the action at one of the noisy tables.

The bartender slid the drink across the bar. His

157

eyes bugged at the size of the roll Liddell pulled from his pocket. He picked up the twenty Liddell dropped on the bar. "This the smallest you got, boss?"

Liddell nodded. "Don't worry about breaking it. I may not be taking any change."

The bartender grunted, took the twenty down to the cash register, rang it up and brought back a small pile of bills and change. He laid it alongside Liddell's drink.

The private detective picked a bill off the pile, passed it across the bar. "Have a drink on me."

The bartender ran the flat of his hand across his bald pate, nodded. "Thanks." He picked the bill up, stuck it in his pocket. "You a stranger in town, boss?"

Liddell nodded. "Been on the Coast for the last couple years." He tasted his drink, grimaced. "They're using more fusel oil these days."

The bartender shrugged. "I only work here, boss."

"Not much going. This town used to jump."

"That's for sure, boss. I like to remember when the Cotton Club and Dickey Wells were running. Mammy's Kitchen over on Lenox Avenue. They're all gone." His teeth gleamed whitely against the dark skin. "Man, but them were times."

"How does a guy get action?"

The smile faded, the bartender shook his head.

"Might be able to steer you to a stag. Something like that. Rest of the town's tight. They scared the ofays off coming up here. It's not like the old days."

Liddell leaned across the bar, dropped his voice. "Look. What I really need is a connect. My man went down in front of the gun. I'm getting in a real panic."

"Can't help you out there none, man." He glanced around the room. "We just get the lushers, no heads. The gold done clamped down tight up here. You got your own spike, you might make a connect with a pusher up at Sammy's. That's an all night cafeteria on 130th. That's the best steer I can give you."

"I don't have a spike. I need a gallery."

The bartender caught his lower lip between his teeth. "I know a class joint that hustles. But it costs heavy. It's a private club."

Liddell nodded. "If you can do me good, there's a sawbuck in it for you. You put me next to someone who's holding and I'm not asking for how much a pop."

The white teeth gleamed again. "I'll see what I can do, boss." He shuffled to the end of the bar, picked up a phone and dialed a number. He talked for a moment, seemed to be arguing, then shuffled back.

"You're in, boss. But I'll have to have one of our boys drive you."

Liddell nodded, brought out the roll, picked out a ten. He folded it in his palm, reached over and shook hands with the bartender. When he got his hand back it was empty.

The bartender walked over to the bouncer, whispered to him. The short fat man nodded, pulled back the partition and disappeared through. The bartender returned.

"They'll be a car out front in a few minutes. The driver will know where to take you."

Liddell nodded, lifted the drink, tried to swallow it, couldn't make it.

A black car without lights was waiting out front when Liddell finally left the candy store. A wizened little man, his skin the color of old mahogany, sat behind the wheel. He had a grease-stained chauffeur's hat on the back of his head. He stared at Liddell blandly as he walked up.

"You the driver the bartender made arrangements with?" Liddell stuck his head in the window.

The driver grunted assent. He waited until Liddell got in, settled back against the cushions, then slid the car into gear and headed toward Seventh Avenue. There he swung north to 125th Street, executed a series of right and left turns clumsily designed to confuse Liddell, ended up on a street in what appeared to be the industrial section. A few blocks away Liddell could hear the sounds of the river. The building in front of which they stopped appeared to be a darkened warehouse.

"This is it." The driver spoke his first words since Liddell had gotten into the car. His voice was surprisingly heavy for so wizened a frame.

"This? But I thought——"

The driver swung around on his seat. "What'd you expect? Neon lights and a brass band? You wanted Matty Lou's, right?" He indicated the dark façade of the warehouse. "This is Matty Lou's. You don't like the look of it, I'll take you back where I picked you up." The tone of his voice made it clear he didn't care one way or the other.

CHAPTER 17

During the day,
the street was undoubtedly clogged with heavy trucks
lumbering toward the river. But at this hour of the
morning it was deserted, lined on either side by dark,
hulking warehouses. For the entire length of the
block only three street lamps spilled yellow light into
the gutter, light that spread like a puddle from
the curbs to the buildings, leaving the alleyways and
the doorways in deep shadow.

Liddell watched the taillight of the car that had
brought him as it winked its way toward the far corner, then disappeared. He crossed the sidewalk toward the entrance of the building. Deep in
the shadows he could see a pinpoint of light that
glowed and brightened, then died away.

A tall Negro in a pearl grey fedora that sat high
on his head, its brim parallel to his eyes, stood in the

doorway. His skin was so black as to be invisible in the shadows. He stood sucking on a cigarette.

"Looking for somebody, mistuh?" His voice was harsh, guttural.

"Matty Lou's place."

"You a membuh?"

As his eyes became accustomed to the darkness, Liddell could see that the other man was big, hulking-shouldered, thick-necked. He shook his head. "The bartender at a little spot on 118th Street fixed it up for me. He said it would be all right."

"Ain't nobody can say it's all right less'n it's Matty Lou," the doorman told him sullenly. He reached out, pressed an invisible button. Someplace far away a bell rang.

After what seemed an eternity, Liddell heard the screech of an unoiled door being opened. The doorman caught him by the arm, propelled him into the darkness. The door squealed shut.

The beam of a flashlight split the darkness. It revealed a fat Negress whose flesh seemed to flow and bulge, foreshortened by the height of the doorman. Her eyes were nearly hidden by fatty pouches, her lips were thick. Her small neck was covered with strings of beads.

"Who is this, Leben?" Her voice was blubbery, sounded choked by the fat jowls.

"Says Riva from the candy store okayed him."

163

His eyes were fixed on Liddell. They were small, pig-like; had red where they should have been white. A scar that ran from the side of his eye to the corner of his mouth was grey, dead-looking. "He ain't a mem-buh."

The fat woman bobbed her head, disturbing the rolls of fat that hung from her jowls. "Riva called." She snapped off the flashlight, drenching the place in darkness. "You better get out front, Leben."

Liddell could hear the guard grunt, then the door opened and squealed shut. As soon as the door was closed, the fat woman turned on the flashlight, knifed a path of light through the darkness.

"Follow me."

She led the way across what obviously had once been a huge warehouse space, now unused and dusty, to a flight of metal stairs in the rear. As they reached the staircase, Liddell became aware of a dull, monotonous beat that made the old building vibrate. It grew louder as they climbed the stairs. The woman stopped at a metal door, pulled it open. Behind it a thick black curtain hung from the ceiling to the floor. She pulled it aside, motioned for Liddell to enter.

A cloud of heavily scented smoke rolled out at him, almost smothered him. The muffled beat he had heard coming up the stairs was now identifiable as the pounding of a drum. It was supplemented by the thin whine of a clarinet, the heavy-throated moan of a sax and other instruments he couldn't place. He traced its source to an automatic phonograph in the corner.

The room itself was bathed in a subdued light, all windows were covered with heavy material like that over the door. On the floor a thick blue rug completed the soundproofing and lightproofing.

The room was large, took up half the warehouse floor space. There was no furniture, but a dozen or more couples were sprawled on cushions. The women were for the most part white, the men predominantly black.

A tall brunette danced wildly in the middle of the floor, her hair flying, her body undulating to the wild beat of the music. No one paid her much attention although Liddell readily recognized her as a big name dancing star from a current musical.

Overhead, a sluggish cloud of smoke swirled lazily in the draught from the drawn durtain.

Liddell had almost forgotten the fat woman alongside him until she asked. "Riva tells me you lost your connection?"

"Lucky I ran into him. Next thing I'd be shooting cotton."

She led the way through the sprawling couples. "You missed the community pop but we've got

165

spikes and a layout out here. You can fix your own pop and get up on their cloud." At the far side of the room she opened a door.

Inside there was a fully equipped shooting gallery, with needles soaking in alcohol, piles of cotton pads, all the necessary equipment.

"What's the tariff?"

"Twenty a cap."

Liddell whistled softly. "Pretty steep."

The fat woman's thick lips parted in a smile. "We're not looking for the subway trade. You get a good go here."

Liddell nodded. "Okay. I'm not arguing."

The fat woman held out her hand. "Hand to hand, mister. You're new to me."

"No credit, eh?" Liddell dug the roll from his pocket, peeled off a twenty. "How about some company? I get lonesome."

The fat woman grinned obscenely. "You like 'em nice and tan? We got something real special." She smacked her lips, rolled her eyes. "She's even got a movie star crazy about her."

"Doesn't cost anything to look."

"Cost plenty to touch. Fifty." She watched while Liddell prepared a hypo. "She sends you almost as much as the horse."

"I'd like to meet her."

The fat woman nodded, walked to the door.

"I'll have the fish send her down. Her name's Poppy."
She closed the door behind her.

As soon as she had left, Liddell "blew the shot" in the sink in the lavatory. He soaked the needle in the alcohol, made a puncture in the crook of his elbow, swabbed at it with a cotton pad.

He walked to the door of the gallery, opened it. Across the room a tall girl was stepping in through the curtain. She was tall, café au lait in color. Her straightened hair was cut in a provocative gamin style. As she crossed the room to where he stood, the sway of her breasts traced designs on the silk peasant blouse she wore. She stopped in front of Liddell, turned the full power of her almond eyes on him.

"I'm Poppy." Her voice was low, sent chills up Liddell's spine. "Matty Lou said you wanted to see me."

"I was lonesome. She said you were good company."

The girl shrugged. "You want to go up now or get some mileage from the pop?" She sounded indifferent.

"Let's sit it out awhile. I hear you have a lot of celebrities come here."

"I suppose so." The girl turned, glided in the direction of some pillows against the far wall. The effect from the rear was as satisfying as it had been from the front. Intriguingly rounded buttocks worked languorously against the tight fabric of her skirt. She dropped onto the pillows, patted a place at her side.

Liddell dropped down beside her. From where he sat he could see every couple in the place. Mike Regan wasn't in the room.

"You don't seem very interested," Poppy complained.

Liddell turned to her, found her half-parted lips inches from his. In the subdued light her skin was soft, golden brown, her hair jet, her lips gleaming and soft. Her eyes gave Liddell's face a workout.

"Just looking around," Liddell shrugged.

The girl moved closer to him. "You're not a head. What are you doing here?" she wanted to know.

"What are you talking about?" Liddell rolled up his sleeve, showed her the fresh puncture. There was a slight discoloration around it. "What's that look like?"

Poppy barely wasted a glance on it. "You're not a needle head. Don't you think I've seen enough of them to be able to tell one when I see him?" She studied his face. "You're not a cop or a Fed or the place would have been hit by now. What are you?"

Liddell considered, decided to take a flyer. "You know a regular named Mike Regan? The movie star?"

She stared at him, started to get up, he pulled her back down. "I'm not going to do him any harm. I'm just trying to locate him. His bosses are getting worried."

"Who are you?"

Liddell considered, plunged. "I'm a private cop. I'm working for the company he works for. They want to know where he is, make sure he hasn't been in any trouble."

Poppy looked around. "You must be crazy. If Matty Lou finds out who you are she'll have that gorilla Leben tear you apart. You better get out of here." She broke off as Matty Lou appeared in the doorway, looked around. "Ask me to go upstairs. I might be able to help," she whispered.

Liddell slid his arm around her, pulled her close. Her mouth sought his, her lips worked against his. He could feel her nails digging into his back. Finally, when they broke, he stood up, pulled her to her feet.

"Let's go upstairs, baby."

He followed her to the curtained doorway. Matty Lou watched him approach with a knowing leer. "You can't have a sample without wanting the whole pie, can you?"

Liddell grinned, followed Poppy to the staircase beyond, up a flight to the next story. A man was sitting in a rocking chair listening to a portable radio. He squinted at Poppy as she came up.

"You can use six."

"He still in there?"

The pimp shrugged, turned to Liddell. "That's fifty, mister."

Liddell pulled out the roll, peeled off two twenties and a ten. The man in the rocking chair snatched it with a gnarled hand, stowed it in his pocket. He bent closer to the radio, seemed to lose interest in them.

Poppy pushed open a door, led the way into a corridor that was lined on both sides with curtained cubicles. She held her finger to her lips, stopped at the second cubicle on the right, pulled back the curtain. A man lay sprawled across an unmade bed. His collar was open, his tie tugged halfway down. A heavy stubble of beard dulled the lines of his jaw. He lay on his back, snoring noisily.

"He's higher than a kite," Liddell grunted.

"He's been mainlining since he got here and he hasn't come down off the cloud yet." She walked over to Regan, shook his shoulder. He grunted something, rolled over on his side. "He's never spiked this hard before. When he first started coming here he had only a chicken habit. Now it's a man-sized monkey."

She stuck her head out the curtain, then motioned for Liddell to follow her to the next cubicle. "What are you going to do about him?"

"He's been here all the time?"

Poppy nodded. "He couldn't—" She broke off, put her finger to her lips. "We better not just be talking if Matty Lou comes up."

She unbuttoned the shoulder of the peasant blouse, slid it back. Then she unzipped her skirt, dropped it to the floor, stepped out of it. Her body was a uniform golden brown. Her legs were long, sensuously shaped. Full rounded thighs swelled into high set hips, converged into a narrow waist. Her stomach was flat, her breasts full and round.

She walked close to Liddell, caught his tie, loosened it. She was helping him out of his coat when the curtain was pulled back.

Matty Lou stood in the doorway, an ugly snub-nosed .38 in her hand. Behind her loomed the bulk of the doorman Leben. The muzzle of the .38 was pointed unwaveringly at a point two inches above Liddell's navel.

"What goes on? An audience makes me nervous," he complained.

"This audience could make you dead, fink." She stepped aside, let Leben into the room. "The fish made him as a cop. He's not one of the inspector's men from around here and I don't think he's gold. See who he is."

"You're making a mistake," Liddell told her.

"You made one. The fish has been in this racket

171

for more years than you got hair. He can smell a cop a mile away and he smells you, man."

Leben licked at his lips, his red-rimmed little eyes on the naked girl. He pushed her aside, managed to grab her breast doing it.

The girl swore at him, jumped with fingers clenched. He caught her on the side of the face with the flat of his hand, sent her sprawling.

"High and mighty, ain't you? Think you're too good for me just because a needle-head ofay likes your smell? One of these days——" He started for her again.

"Stop, Leben." Matty Lou's voice cut like a lash. For a split second her attention wavered.

Liddell moved with lightning speed. His right hand swung out in a vicious chop, caught the fat woman at the juncture of trunk and neck. She gave a strangled sob, dropped like a log.

Leben spun, took the picture in with a glance. He twisted the corners of his thick lips up in a caricature of a smile. "You shouldn'ta done that, ofay. Now I got to kill you." He shuffled toward Liddell, long arms dangling at his sides.

He threw a beefy right at Liddell's jaw from the floor. The detective blocked it easily, slammed his right against Leben's jaw. The big man blinked, shuffled close. He feinted with his left again, crossed his right to Liddell's jaw with a speed and co-

172

ordination rare in a man his size. It slammed Liddell back against the wall where he slid to a sitting position. There was a ringing in his ears, the floor seemed to be tilting crazily as he struggled to his knees.

Leben licked his lips in anticipation, stood over him, waited for him to get up. Liddell shook his head, trying to clear it of the cobwebs. He got to one knee, pretended to lose his balance, but got his legs behind him and ploughed his shoulder into the big man's midsection.

Leben roared his rage as the unexpected lunge bowled him over. There was a crash as the big man hit a chair, splintered it, knocked over a towel hamper and another chair. He lay in the debris, swearing angrily.

By the time Leben pulled himself to his feet, Liddell was waiting in a half crouch. The big man shuffled in, apparently impervious to the detective's Sunday punch as it opened an inch long gash on his cheekbone. He threw a hamlike fist at Liddell's head, missed, gasped as the private detective buried his fist to the wrist in his stomach.

Before he could recover and lash out, Liddell scuttled to the left, threw Leben off balance. The red-rimmed eyes glared hatred as Leben tried to regain his earlier advantage. He took an overhand right to the mouth that smashed his lower lip in an attempt to draw Liddell in close where he could use his murderous right. He swung another looping left that Liddell avoided.

The detective kept circling, hoping to get a clear shot at the big man's midsection. Moving as fast as he could to keep out of the way of Leben's paralyzing right, Liddell tripped over a piece of the broken chair, lost his balance. Leben grinned, threw the right. It landed a few inches too high to do the full job but carried enough steam to knock Liddell flat on his back.

Thinking the private detective was helpless, Leben moved in for the kill. He straddled Liddell's body, brought his right foot up to smash in the detective's face. Liddell lashed up with all his remaining strength with his heels, buried them in the big man's groin. Leben's eyes rolled back, saliva drooled down his chin. He clamped both hands to his midsection, swayed for a moment, then hit the floor face first. He didn't move.

Liddell got to his feet, leaned against the wall to clear his head. The girl came over, slid her arm around him, led him to the bed.

"You're quite a man. Nobody ever went up against Leben before. But don't push your luck. You've got to get out of here." She took his pocket handkerchief, wiped some blood off his chin. "Take Regan with you."

Liddell stared at her. "I'm lucky if I can get out myself. How can I lug a dead weight like him with me?"

"There's an escape hatch at the end of the corridor. It opens in another building and brings you out around the corner. I'll show you the way. Will you?"

Liddell considered. He nodded to the unconscious man on the floor. "What'll happen to you when he finds out?"

The girl got up, walked over to where Leben lay, spat in his face. "I'm not afraid of him. Not any more." She looked up at Liddell. "I could have left with Mike a long time ago. But Matty Lou told me she'd send Leben after me if I ever left her. They used me to bleed Mike. But I'm not afraid any more."

Liddell nodded. "Okay, baby, I'll help." He stood up, grinned at her nakedness. "But maybe you ought to put something on. We're likely to attract too much attention like that."

Johnny Liddell
dragged himself out of bed at eleven the next morning, stumbled into the bathroom, stood under an ice cold shower until he was almost sure he was going to live. The shower eased most of the soreness in his muscles, chilled him into a reasonable degree of wakefulness. He swabbed himself dry with a heavy towel, tied it around his midsection, studied his face in the mirror.

Aside from a slight swelling on the side of his jaw, there was no visible evidence of the tough day he had put in the day before. He stared at his face for a minute, shook his head.

"It'd sure take a brave man to let a red-eyed maniac like you get close to their neck with a razor this morning," he growled at his image. He decided to let the barber in the basement complete his toilet.

After a shave and massage he felt more up to what lay ahead. He decided it would be faster to walk crosstown to Radio City than to buck the slow moving traffic that clogs the crosstown streets between ten in the morning and eight in the night in that area.

At Rockefeller Plaza he crossed to the Associated Press Building, stopped for a minute before going in to read the latest flashes on the recessed news tickers that flank the entrance. There was nothing new on the Carter killing on the twelve o'clock news, just a rehash of the story that had appeared in the morning tabs. The police and the district attorney were still concentrating on the theory that the publisher had been killed in an attempted robbery or kidnaping.

Inside the building, the tenant register showed that S. Minelli Enterprises occupied the 14th floor. The elevator deposited him in the reception room of the Minelli Enterprises.

It was a large room filled with young hopefuls and oldsters who already bore the stamp of despair. They lined the upholstered benches that ran the length of one side of the room.

A railing cut the room in two. Behind it, a girl with patently bleached hair presided over a switchboard, was presently engrossed in a movie magazine. On the walls, giant-sized pictures of Hollywood and

Broadway stars were recessed in indirectly lighted frames.

Liddell crossed to the railing, the blonde took her time about acknowledging his presence. Finally, she glanced up, her jaws working rhythmically on her gum.

"I want to see Minelli," Liddell told her.

She eyed him with no show of enthusiasm. "You mean Mr. Minelli?"

"I mean Sal Minelli."

The blonde looked past him, let her eyes flick along the people sitting on the benches. "What did you think they were doing, waiting for a bus?"

Liddell scowled at her. "Why don't you save the humor for a talent scout and tell your boss I'm here? Tell him it's Johnny Liddell."

The girl at the switchboard started to retort, shrugged elaborately. She jabbed at a key on the board, muttered into the headset. Then she nodded, cut the key.

"You can go in."

She released the catch on the gate in the railing, went back to her movie magazine.

Sal Minelli was perched on the corner of a highly polished desk when Liddell walked in. Lounging in a chair, his legs extended full length in front of him, was the crooner, Tony DeSales. The dark-haired girl who acted as his secretary sat on a leather couch on the far side of the room.

Liddell looked around, grinned. "Old home week."

Minelli rolled an unlit cigar between thumb and forefinger in the center of his mouth, wetting it with his lips. He waited until Liddell closed the door behind him.

"What's on your mind, Liddell?"

"Long time no see. I got lonesome for you, Sal."

"I hadn't noticed." Minelli was lean, affected carefully tailored suits that showed an understanding with his tailor. His hair was beginning to grey, was worn in a closely clipped brush cut. He turned to DeSales. "This the guy?"

The crooner nodded.

Minelli turned back to Liddell. "I hear you've been bothering the kid. You saved me the trouble of sending for you. I thought maybe you ought to get straightened out."

"That's interesting. And who was going to do that?"

Minelli took the cigar from between his teeth, examined the damp end. "I imagine there must be plenty of people around who'd be glad to oblige." He looked up at Liddell. "I don't like people who use my name to get in to see my clients."

179

"Me? Use your name? I'd have to wash my mouth out with soap." He looked over to the girl. "Did I use Mr. Minelli's name?"

The girl shook her head. "I just assumed you were from him. You said you were trying to keep Tony's name out of the Carter case."

"And why would you want to do that?" Minelli asked softly.

"Not for him, that's for sure. And certainly not for you."

"But?"

"When Carter was knocked off, a lot of material from his files disappeared. Material that can do a lot of people a lot of harm."

"You still didn't tell me why you're interested."

"Celeste Pierce."

Minelli raised his eyebrows. "A nice piece of goods."

"Also a client."

"All that and a fee, too. So why come to me? What do you want, congratulations?"

Liddell grinned tightly. "No. I just wanted to pass the word along that she's a client. And I don't like my clients bothered."

Minelli pulled the cigar from between his teeth. "Sounds tough. What's it mean?" Tight little lumps formed on the sides of the agent's jaw.

"It means if somebody bugs my client for anything, I bug back. But hard."

The man on the desk squinted at him. "You're making with big sounds, but you're not getting to me. You got something to tell me, spill it. Otherwise, I got work to do."

"Carter wasn't killed in a heist or a snatch. You know that and I know it."

"So what's it to me?"

"Carter was giving a property of yours a bad time. This creep."

The crooner started to pull himself to his feet, Minelli waved him back. "So what's it to you?"

"When he was killed, Carter had some material and art on my client. It disappeared. The killer got it."

"Sad."

"The killer can't unload it without fingering himself for the job. But maybe he's got other uses for it than to publish it."

Minelli shrugged. "So what's the problem? If he can't publish it, maybe your client can do business with whoever has it."

"I don't think we'd like to do business on those terms."

"What terms?"

Liddell walked over to a leather chair, dropped

into it. "Carter never used the article he had set on DeSales, did he?"

The man on the desk flicked a quick glance at the crooner. DeSales tried to meet his eyes, didn't manage it. "Who says he had an article on the kid?"

"I do. The article never ran and right about that time, DeSales came into your stable. Coincidence, wasn't it?"

The agent hopped off the corner of the desk, walked over to where DeSales was busily examining his hands in his lap. "Where did this shamus get that pipe dream?"

DeSales looked up, spread his hands palms up. "Look, Sal, I didn't——"

Minelli's hand swung in a short arc, knocked the crooner's head to the side. "You talk too much, kid." He nodded to the girl. "Get him out of here. I'll talk to him later."

The girl unfolded her legs from the couch, walked over to where DeSales sat, his hand to his cheek. "Come on, Tony. We have a two o'clock show to do."

Minelli waited until they had left the room, walked back to Liddell. "You trying to make something of it, shamus?"

Liddell shrugged. "I just said it's quite a coincidence."

"No coincidence. That's what an agent's for. To get his clients out of trouble." He stared at Liddell with expressionless eye. "Also to keep them out of trouble." He pulled the cigar from between his teeth, pointed it at Liddell. "Look, I don't like you. I don't like no part of you. But I'm going to give you some advice. Free."

"That's nice."

"If that client of yours is on the hook for some pictures and an article, sending you to throw your muscle around is no way to make friends. And she's going to need friends. All the friends she can get."

"That the advice? That she should change her deodorant?"

Minelli snarled at him. "If I was managing her——"

"Which you're not."

Some of the anger drained from Minelli's face. "You never know in this business, do you, shamus?"

Liddell reached over to a leather-topped table next to his chair, helped himself to a cigarette.

"Be my guest," Minelli snarled. He stamped around, dropped into the chair behind the desk, scowled while Liddell lit the cigarette with a silver table lighter. "Is there anything else I can get you?"

"You were saying?"

"I was saying that if I was her manager, I'd try

to act nicer to people and maybe the people who have the pictures might give her a way to get them back."

"That's what I thought you said."

"Look at it this way. A studio gets to tie up a lot of dough in a property like Pierce. They stand to blow a bundle if word gets out how she used to make her bread and butter in the old days. A smart agent might be able to show them how to save their investment instead of throwing her out on her can."

"And if she doesn't have a smart agent?"

Minelli shrugged. "Then she hasn't a dream. Those pictures will show up and she's washed up."

"Is that a promise or a threat?"

"Look. You came here, I didn't send for you. If I had, you wouldn't be sitting there smoking my cigarettes, making with the small talk. You want to save your client a real headache, you get her a smart agent."

"And you're a smart agent."

"The smartest."

Liddell considered it, nodded. "Suppose my client did join your stable?"

"The pictures and the article would never be published."

"And what does it cost her to have the privilege of your advice and guidance?"

Minelli studied his fingernails. "Thirty per cent of the gross."

Liddell grunted. "That's a pretty rich cut, isn't it? Most agents take ten per cent."

"Depends on what you get from an agent. On a property like this, there are a lot of extra expenses, a lot of hidden costs that I have to absorb. We give our clients, in a case like this, a lot more than they can buy from any other agent in the business."

"Suppose she signs up and a year from now the pictures pop up again?"

Minelli smiled bleakly. "When we take on a client, we make an investment in that client. We don't like people who make our investments a bad risk."

"We?"

"Yeah, we. Me and my associates." He leaned his forearms on the desk. "You see those pictures outside? All clients. You ever read anything about any of them in a rag like Carter put out?"

"Maybe they kept their noses clean."

"Don't make me laugh. I've got more adult delinquents on my books than any other agent. But as long as they're my property, nobody is going to bugger them." He pulled open the top drawer of his desk, pulled out a blank form. "That client of yours ought to look at it this way—seventy per cent of her present

185

take is a helluva lot better than ninety per cent of nothing." He flipped the form across the desk. "Have her sign this."

Liddell looked it over. "It's not filled in."

"Don't you trust me?"

"No."

Minelli grinned. "So don't do business with me. I give your client a real chance for an out. If you don't want it, don't take it. But don't say I didn't give her a chance."

"I'll talk to her about it." Liddell folded the form, put it in his pocket.

Minelli leaned back. "She's a very photogenic girl, that client of yours. It will be a pleasure to do business with her." He grinned at Liddell's back as the private detective walked toward the door.

Liddell stopped with his hand on the knob. "Maybe Carter's kill wasn't too good an idea from your point of view. Without him to soften them up you may find it harder to get new clients or even keep the ones you've now got on the hook."

CHAPTER 19

At 2:45,
Johnny Liddell pushed open the plate-glass door to
his office. Pinky swung around on her chair, glared
at him.

"Why don't you ever check in? How do I know
what you're doing or where to reach you if I need
you?"

"Since when do you need me? It was my impression that you ran this whole operation."

"Very funny." She consulted her desk pad. "You
know anyone named Matty Regis? He's called four
times today already."

"Leave a number?"

"He didn't know where he could be reached.
Said he'd be in and out all day. He'll try to reach you.
Inspector Herlehy wants you to call him." She looked
up. "Want me to get him?"

"No. If he calls, you still haven't heard from me." He pushed through the gate, started for the private office.

"Oh, I forgot to tell you. You've got company."

Liddell turned around, frowned. "Who?"

"Our client. The Rexall redhead. She's been waiting for over an hour." She nodded toward the private office. "I put her in there so every elevator boy in the building wouldn't be taking shortcuts through our office."

Liddell grunted, walked into the inner office. The redhead was sitting behind his desk, working at her nails. She looked up as he entered and smiled. She got up, came around the desk, threw her arms around him, glued her body to his.

"Johnny, are you all right?"

He held her away. "As far as I know I'm still on my feet."

"You're not in any trouble?" She studied the perplexed frown on his face. "When I heard about Les Ringer—" She broke off. "You knew he was dead?"

"Where and when?"

"They found his body this morning in an alley on the East Side." She grinned ruefully. "I got scared. I remembered that when I asked you for help you wanted to know who I wanted killed. I knew you were kidding but when I heard about Ringer——"

"Don't worry about it, baby. I didn't kill Ringer." He walked around the desk, dug the bottle out of the bottom drawer. "Wish I could offer you something, baby, but I've only got bourbon."

"I don't need it. Just knowing you're in the clear is all the lift I need." The redhead walked over to the customer's chair, sat down and crossed her legs. "Who do you suppose killed Les?"

Liddell tilted the bottle over a glass, spilled in two fingers of liquor. "I don't know, but it's narrowing down." He walked over to where a cooler was muttering to itself against the wall, softened the bourbon with water. "You're not the only one Ringer did a piece on for Carter."

Celeste watched him recross the room to his desk chair. "Who else?"

"Slugger Ryan, movie actor Mike Regan and this crooner, Tony DeSales." He took a deep swallow from the glass, made concentric rings with its wet bottom on his blotter. "Any one of them would have had the motive."

"You think that's why Les was killed? Because he was digging dirt for Carter?"

"It figures. If Carter was killed for publishing it, why not kill the guy who was feeding the stuff to him to make the cover complete?"

The redhead fumbled through her bag, came up with a pack of cigarettes, stuck one between her lips. "What did it say about DeSales? I don't remember that one."

"The article didn't run. That's the interesting part about it. Carter was apparently giving the kid a bad time, then when the time came for the article to run"—he dug Les Ringer's memo book from his pocket—"that was last February, it didn't run. And it hasn't run since."

"Why?"

Liddell drained the glass, put the bottle and the glass back in the bottom drawer. "That's what I wanted to know. So I asked DeSales about it."

"Would he tell you?"

Liddell grinned. "He was a little reluctant at first, but then he opened up all the way. There was a fix."

"He paid off?"

"In a way. But not for money. And not by bird-dogging other articles for Carter."

Celeste frowned. "How then?"

"He agreed to sign a management contract. With Sal Minelli."

"And the article didn't appear?"

Liddell nodded. "Just like that." He drew the blank form from his breast pocket, passed it across the desk to the girl. "Would you sign that contract, baby?"

She looked at it, turned it over. She stared up at Liddell. "As is?"

He nodded.

"But it's blank. They could fill in anything they wanted."

"Suppose, like DeSales, that was the price of getting your material back."

The redhead caught her lower lip between her teeth. "Is it?"

Liddell shook his head. "Not if I have anything to say about it. I would like to know whether or not Minelli has that material, though. If it was there when you left and gone when I got there——"

"But why should Minelli kill Carter?"

Liddell leaned back, laced his fingers at the back of his neck. "Let's say Carter had the job of softening up prospective clients for Sal Minelli. You, for instance. Mike Regan for another. Tony DeSales for another. That represents some important dough."

"Okay, let's say that."

"In DeSales' case, everything went okay. De-Sales was going to get taken apart by Carter. He made the deal with Minelli, the story was dropped. According to Ringer's notes——"

"Where did you get Ringer's notes? I thought you said——"

"I paid him a visit when he wasn't home. I

thought he might have the material. He didn't have, but I found this." He dug the memo book up, held it out. "It has his notes for the four articles, how much he got paid, and when they were supposed to run. The only one that ran on schedule was Slugger Ryan's. DeSales' was cancelled, Regan's hadn't run yet. Yours was due in the current issue."

"You still haven't told me why Minelli should kill him."

"Suppose Carter saw a chance to make a killing on his own. Without Minelli." He paused for a moment. "Suppose Minelli, Ringer and Carter were working this dodge. Ringer did the digging, Carter softened the prospect up by threatening to run the piece, and Minelli put on the clincher by signing the mark to a foolproof contract."

"So?"

"In your case, Carter realizes he can sell millions of magazines, clean up on that one issue. So instead of softening you up, he uses the cackle bladder routine because he intends to run the story and cross Minelli up? How do you think Sal would react?"

The redhead shrugged. "He'd probably flip."

"Don't let the fancy office and the pretty clothes fool you. In the old days, Minelli was a tough baby. He did a lot of his talking with a .45. Crossing him is no way to grow old gracefully."

"And Ringer?"

"He got caught in the middle. An old operator like Minelli wouldn't want to leave anyone around who might crack and tie Minelli to the Carter kill. Les called me last night, told me he thought he could finger the killer for me. But first he wanted to talk it over with another interested party. He didn't keep the date with me."

"But he could have meant Slugger Ryan or Mike Regan or even DeSales himself."

"For that matter, it's entirely possible that there's no connection at all between Carter's murder and Ringer's killing," Liddell grunted.

"But you don't believe that?"

Liddell pursed his lips, shook his head slowly. "It's a little too coincidental for my blood. No, I think they were both murdered by the same person and for the same reason."

"And that would mean it had to be related to the magazine."

"It figures. I can tie Ringer to Carter by this memo book of his. The next thing I've got to do is tie Minelli to Carter. Then I think we can start tying the loose ends of this thing together."

"How can you tie Minelli to Carter?"

Liddell picked up a pencil, doodled on the yellow pad for a moment. "My only hope is Carter's editor, Bob Hunter. He may be able to establish some tie between them."

193

"How?"

Liddell shrugged. "It's a long shot. But maybe he had to run an errand to Minelli's or maybe he's seen Minelli up at the penthouse. If I can just latch onto one thread like that I may be able to make somebody start spilling."

The redhead took a last puff on her cigarette, crushed it out. "Look, Johnny, I got you into this. For my sake be careful. The killer has already killed two people. Don't let him make it an even three." She got up, walked over to where he sat, bent over and covered his mouth with hers. "Getting the pictures and material back wouldn't be worth that."

Pinky picked that moment to push the door open. "Sorry. I didn't know you were itemizing the bill," she chirped. "That Matty Regis is on the phone. Want to take it? This one might be a cash deal," she added sweetly.

Liddell scowled at her. "I'll take it. And from now on, knock."

"Yes, sir. I just figured you wouldn't hear me if I pounded." She tossed a smile in the redhead's direction, made a production of closing the door after her.

"Quaint little character," Celeste murmured. "I suppose you keep her around for atmosphere."

The buzz of the phone eliminated the necessity

for an answer. Liddell grabbed the receiver and held it to his ear. "Liddell."

"This is Matty Regis, Liddell. I'm vice-president in charge of public relations for Magna Pictures. I understand we owe you a fee."

Liddell reached for a cigarette in the pack on the desk. "What for?"

"I understand you did quite a job for us last night. This morning, rather. Our mutual friend is resting incognito over at Roosevelt Hospital. That's why I haven't been in my office all day."

"Oh, that."

There was a slight pause. "I suppose you know that the Federal men raided a dope joint in Harlem early this morning. It's in all the late papers. Made quite a haul."

"You don't owe me anything, Regis."

Regis chuckled softly. "That's what you think. They would have made a much bigger haul if they had knocked it over a couple of hours earlier. We owe you plenty."

Liddell grinned. "Forget it. They wouldn't have hit it at all if they hadn't gotten one of those anonymous tips on it." He tapped a thin collar of ash in the ashtray. "I was up there for another client. What happened with your friend was just incidental."

"Good. Then when you get our check tomorrow

enter it in your books under incidentals. I hope five hundred dollars will cover it."

"Look—"

The voice on the other end cut him off. "You were up there pretending to be working for us. If you hadn't done a good job, we would have complained. We think you did a good job and we insist on paying for it."

Liddell shrugged. "Mister, be my guest."

"Thanks for everything." The phone on the other end went dead. Liddell stared at the receiver, dropped it on the hook.

"Bad news?" the redhead wanted to know anxiously.

"Not unless you call parlaying a dime into a five century note bad luck." He pushed a button on the base of the phone. He scowled a minute later when it sounded as if someone were trying to knock down the door. "Come in," he roared.

Pinky pushed the door open, looked from one to the other. "Somebody ring?"

"You know damn well I did. Make out a card for Magna Pictures. Check coming in tomorrow by mail."

Pinky frowned. "What did we do for them?"

"Made a telephone call."

CHAPTER 20

Bob Hunter,
editor of *Bare Facts,* sat behind his cluttered desk,
swabbed at his bald pate with a circular motion of
his handkerchief. He jumped apprehensively at the
sound of a knock on the outer office door, debated
the advisability of not answering it, lost the decision.

He crossed the inner office into the cluttered
anteroom. "Who is it?" he asked cautiously.

"Liddell. Johnny Liddell."

Hunter unlocked the door, peered out. When
he recognized the private detective he pulled the
door all the way open. "Come in." He locked the
door after Liddell, led the way into his office.

"Busy?" Liddell grinned.

The editor walked around his desk, dropped
heavily into his chair. The silver bristle on his chin
was heavier, the bristling eyebrows seemed even more
ferocious.

"Yeah," he grunted. "Busy trying to stay alive."

Liddell dug a pack of cigarettes from his pocket, tilted two out, offered one to the man behind the desk. Hunter took it, wet the end with his tongue before placing it in his mouth.

"What's that supposed to mean?" Liddell pulled a chair up to the desk, sat down. "Busy trying to stay alive?"

Hunter squinted at him. "You kidding? There's two down and one to go. That one is me." He touched a match to the cigarette, drew a lungful of smoke, exhaled it in twin streams through his nostrils. "And I'm in no hurry to round out the three."

"Don't tell me you're superstitious."

"Look, Liddell, nobody's kidding me. Not even me. I see the handwriting on the wall. Somebody's out to get even for what this rag did to them. They got the guy who published it, they got the guy who wrote it. Don't you think they're going to be real neat and get the guy who edited it?"

"It had occurred to me," Liddell conceded. His cigarette hung in the corner of his mouth where it waggled when he talked. "It has also occurred to me that the killer doesn't have to get to you or anybody else."

"How?"

Liddell shrugged. "Help me get at him before he does."

198

"How do I do that?"

"Open up." Liddell studied the face of the man opposite him for a moment. "You know something that could help me to get him." He held his hand up, cut off an objection. "Maybe you know it and just don't realize its importance."

Hunter raked back the long hairs over his ears with clenched fingers. "You think I wouldn't spill if I knew who it was or why he was killing? My life isn't very fancy but it's the only one I've got and I'd like to hang onto it for a while."

"Well, the best way to do that is to start remembering the answers to a couple of questions."

"Such as?"

"Les Ringer fed Carter a lot of stuff for the magazine. Right?"

The editor bobbed his head.

"You knew what was scheduled. This business of you not knowing what inventory Carter had on hand was for the birds. Right?"

Hunter sucked on his cigarette, considered. "I knew what articles were coming up. I had no copies of them. What I told you about Carter keeping all the galleys was true. He okayed them just before they were skedded and I took them from there."

Liddell nodded. "Okay. Now, let's get back to Tony DeSales. Carter had an article on him. It would have put the kid out of business. Why didn't it run?"

Hunter shrugged. "That's one I can't answer."

"But that's the big one."

Hunter shook his head. "I don't know. It was skedded but Carter pulled it at the last minute and substituted one on the Marissoff girl."

"Any kickback on that one?"

Hunter made a face. "That screwball? She loved the publicity. I'll bet she bought up a dozen copies and sent them to her dyke friends all over the world."

Liddell got up, walked over to the window, looked down into the littered air shaft. "You know that right after that article was killed Tony DeSales became a client of Sal Minelli?"

"No."

Liddell swung around. "Do you know Minelli?"

The editor nodded. "I know who he is. A big shot agent."

"Do you know whether or not Carter knew Minelli?"

"He might have. He knew almost everybody. Or something about them."

"Think hard, Hunter. Did you ever see Minelli at Carter's penthouse? At any time?"

Hunter sucked deeply on his cigarette, shook his head slowly. "No."

"Did you ever go to Minelli's office for Carter? Bring him something? Some proofs or a message? Anything like that?"

"What is this with Minelli? Where does he fit?"

Liddell grinned mirthlessly, walked back to the desk. "You want me to cancel out the guy that's trying to make it an even three, don't you? So I'm asking a couple of questions that might help me do it."

"But where would Minelli fit in this? Carter never did a piece on him. He'd be too smart to go up against a character like Minelli. Everybody knows he's no cream puff."

"Right. Let me tell you what a little broad said to me the other day. She said do you think when they run an article tearing somebody's reputation to pieces that person's the only one they hurt? How about the people who love him? How about the people who have an investment in him?"

Hunter tried to meet Liddell's eyes, dropped his. He picked up a fresh cigarette, chain lit it from the butt. "I never claimed it was anything but a filthy business." He crushed out the spent butt. "A lot of people get hurt. Innocent people."

"Okay. Does that answer your question about where Minelli fits?"

The editor looked up, squinted at Liddell through the smoke. "Not entirely. So DeSales was his client and he didn't get hurt." He scratched at the side of his jaw. "I suppose what you're getting at is that Carter and Minelli had a deal to build Minelli a stable."

Liddell nodded. "That's what I'm getting at. Celeste Pierce was the next property to get the softening-up touch."

"Celeste Pierce, eh?" Hunter pursed his lips. "Then why the elaborate frame to make it look like she shot him? Why give the printer orders to be ready to make an extra run?"

Liddell shrugged. "A double cross maybe. Instead of softening her up and turning her over to Minelli for the treatment, he decided to sell a million extra copies."

"Minelli could get a little peeved if that happened," Hunter conceded. "But where did it get him? He still doesn't have Pierce and the material is gone. She's the only one that benefits." He looked up quickly at Liddell, looked away.

"What's that mean?"

The editor smoked with short nervous puffs. "Nothing. It—it just sort of popped out. I just meant that Pierce really gets a break. Carter is dead, so is Les Ringer and the material is missing. She's really in the clear."

Liddell walked around the desk, caught the man by his lapels, pulled him to his feet. "You implying that maybe I did it?"

Perspiration beaded the editor's forehead, his eyes shot from side to side. "No," he protested. "No."

Liddell pushed him back into the chair. "I know just what you're thinking. Yesterday I told you I intended to have a talk with Ringer, this morning he turns up dead." He crushed the cigarette out in the ash tray. "There's only one trouble. If I had killed Carter I'd have the damned material and I wouldn't be knocking myself out trying to get it back."

Hunter dug the handkerchief from his hip pocket, swabbed at his forehead and pate. "I didn't think of that." His eyes avoided Liddell's. "Who do you think has the material?"

"Minelli."

The editor's eyes snapped up to Liddell's face. "That would put the finger on him as the killer. What makes you think that?"

"An agent is a guy who gets things for his clients. I think Minelli is the kind of an agent who spares them things." He leaned the flat of both hands on the desk. "I think we're going to find out that more than one of his clients are in his stable for that reason."

"You're just guessing."

Liddell shook his head. "No. Not just guessing. He gave me a contract to be signed by my client. It's a blank contract. He fills it in to suit himself."

The editor stared at him. "And what does he guarantee in return?"

Liddell grinned bleakly. "That the pictures and the material will never show up. If she doesn't sign, he can almost guarantee that they will."

"Then he must have them."

"That's the way I figure. Now all I need is a tie between him and Carter. And you're the only one that can give me that."

The editor ran the tips of his fingers along the silvery stubble on his chin. "I wish I could. But I can't." He wrinkled his forehead. "I don't remember ever seeing them together. I don't remember ever hearing Carter mention Minelli. And I've certainly never been to his office."

Liddell shrugged. "Like I said, it was a long shot." He nodded to the editor. "I hope Minelli doesn't suddenly remember some way you can tie him to Carter. He might decide to wipe the slate clean."

CHAPTER 21

In the lobby
of 1660 Broadway, Johnny Liddell stepped into a phone booth, dialed the number of his office. On the third ring, the voice of his secretary came on.

"Johnny Liddell's office."

"This is Liddell. What's doing?"

"I've been trying to reach you. The district attorney's office has been calling you. They don't sound very happy."

"What do they want?"

"You."

"Who called?"

There was a slight pause while she consulted her pad. "An assistant D.A. named Marcus. He didn't sound very happy."

"What the hell does he want? They gave me seventy-two hours. I've got twenty-four left."

"He didn't confide in me," the girl told him

sweetly. "He just told me to tell you to get down there *tout de suite* or he'd send someone to get you."

Liddell growled under his breath. "Anything else?"

"Yes. Just one thing. A personal favor."

"What's that?"

"Tell your girl friend to change her brand. I've been busy ever since you left airing the office out. She's a little overpowering and I don't mean just physically."

Liddell snorted. "That perfume costs sixty bucks an ounce."

"I guess you should know." There was a faint click and the line was broken.

Liddell slammed his receiver on the hook, stalked out of the booth. He waved down a cruising cab, gave the driver the address of the district attorney's office. The cabby tried to draw him into conversation, Liddell fended him off with a grunt. After a few tries, the cabby gave it up, took it out on a few inoffensive pedestrians whom he sent scuttling in all directions. The only real satisfaction he derived from the trip was the shouted comments on his driving when he made a two wheeled left turn in front of a truck which left the driver standing on his brake.

Upstairs, Johnny Liddell was kept waiting almost fifteen minutes in one of the anterooms adjoining Marcus Jacobs's office. He had finished his second cigarette, was considering the advisability of leaving when Inspector Herlehy of Homicide walked into the office.

"I've been trying to reach you all day," Herlehy growled at him. "Don't you ever go to your office?"

Liddell shrugged. "Not when I'm on a job that takes twenty-four hours a day."

Herlehy pounded on his gum. "Then you can start relaxing. You're off the job." He walked to the door to Jacobs's office, opened it, stuck his head in. Then he turned, nodded to Liddell. "Let's go."

Jacobs was slumped disconsolately in his chair when Herlehy and the private detective walked in. He greeted them both with a bilious glare. "Sit down."

Herlehy found a leather chair, Liddell dropped into the chair in front of the D.A.'s desk.

"What's this all about?" He looked from the D.A. to Herlehy and back. "We had a deal I was to get seventy-two hours. I've got at least twenty-four to go."

Jacobs clapped the palm of his hand to his forehead. "Another twenty-four hours he wants. In another twenty-four hours I'll be back mailing out circulars for the twenty-third A. D."

"What's going on?"

He looked to Herlehy with stricken eyes. "What's going on? he wants to know." His eyes rolled back to Liddell. "You got any idea how many reporters are trying to break this door down? You got any idea how much heat they're putting on the old man?"

Liddell shrugged. "That was part of the deal. Hold them off for three days and then you'll have some red meat to give them."

"The deal's off," Jacobs told him with finality. "No more deal."

"That's crazy. You think you've got heat now because a couple of reporters are giving you a hot foot? How hot do you think it's going to get when the high powered P.R. men from the studios start to yell for your scalp for ruining their pet properties?"

Jacobs groaned. "You already sold us that bill of goods. Remember? What's it got us so far?"

Liddell dug a sheet of yellow foolscap from his breast pocket. "Here's what it's gotten you. I've been able to eliminate a half a dozen people who had good reason to kill Carter but not the opportunity. And they're people like Mike Regan of Magna Pictures, Sonny Morris who's got connections up to here. People like that."

Jacobs licked at his lips, managed to look pacified. "But how many haven't you cleared?"

"I've got four live possibles."

Herlehy nodded. "They're the ones I'm interested in. Not the ones that couldn't have done it. Who are they?"

"Tony DeSales."

The assistant D.A. scowled. "Who?" He looked to Herlehy for explanation.

"He's that crooner the kids are all crazy about. A vicious little hood with a record as long as your arm. For assault."

Liddell nodded. "Carter had an article set on him. But it never ran. He has Sal Minelli as his manager. Minelli became his manager just before the article was due to run."

Herlehy pursed his lips. "Who else?"

"Slugger Ryan. He threatened to get Carter and maybe he did. I tried to talk to him, got a clout in the jaw for my trouble. His manager Leo Dugan let the word around that Carter'd get his if he took another crack at Ryan. So Carter was readying another article that implied that Dugan had fixed Ryan's last fight."

Jacobs groaned. "We know all about Dugan. He's been throwing his weight around down at the Hall. If you finger his boy, you'd better be able to back it up. Because you're strictly on your own."

Liddell grinned crookedly. "But if I can bring him in all wrapped up in tissue paper you're with me?"

"Let's get some coffee in here, Mark," Herlehy broke in. He waited while the D.A. pushed a button. A uniformed patrolman stuck his head in, took the order, withdrew.

"Who else is on the possible list?" Herlehy turned to Liddell.

"A Cafe Society character named Marissoff. She——"

"Scratch her," Herlehy grunted. "She's been in the can on a disorderly conduct charge since Monday. The vice boys knocked over a dyke joint in the Village and she was Queen of the May."

"So according to your list, that leaves only three possible," the assistant D.A. grunted. He tabulated them on his finger. "Tony DeSales the crooner, Slugger Ryan and Leo Dugan. Oh, that's just fine. Just fine." He turned to Herlehy. "You see? You try to level with these guys, you see what happens?"

Liddell looked from one to the other, got nothing from their faces. "What's that supposed to mean?"

"You know there are more than three possibles," Herlehy growled at him. "What kind of a smokescreen do you think you're throwing up?"

"Smokescreen?"

The patrolman came in, deposited three containers of coffee on the desk, withdrew. When he had closed the door behind him, Liddell met Herlehy's glance levelly.

"I just asked you, Inspector. What do you mean by smokescreen?"

The inspector reached over, snagged a container of coffee, rolled it between his palms. "You forgot to include your client's name, didn't you, Liddell?"

"I thought we'd eliminated her."

Jacobs leaned forward. "You must think this department is run by a bunch of damn fools. You should have known that phony alibi wouldn't stand in the face of an autopsy." He scowled while Liddell helped himself to a container of coffee. "Your client has an alibi that starts at three. And you gave it to her."

Liddell gouged the top from his container, stirred the coffee with his forefinger. "The inspector himself says Carter was alive at four-thirty."

"You were counting on that, weren't you, Liddell? How could you have been so sure that an alibi at three would stand up? Did you know about the phone call at four-thirty? That Carter was already dead over an hour by then?"

"You told me. Remember? What suddenly makes you so sure he was dead before then?"

"Because we know what he ate at eleven-thirty and the contents of his stomach prove he was dead no more than three hours later, probably less," Jacobs put in. "That puts your client right back in the middle of it."

"My client didn't kill Carter," Liddell asserted.

"Did you?" Herlehy wanted to know.

There was a significant pause. "Would you like to try to prove that, Inspector?"

"Somebody was in Carter's room at four-thirty and answered the phone. If it wasn't you, who was it?"

"The man who got Carter's files, including the material on my client probably."

Herlehy snorted. He jabbed the top of his container open, took a swallow and burned his tongue. He swore fluently.

"I can't prove it was you in that room yet, Liddell," Jacobs told him in a hard voice. "I do know you've been crossing this office ever since this case broke. And we're not going to forget it when the time comes to renew that paper of yours."

"Look, Jacobs, you think what you want to think. I know you're getting plenty of heat and you're looking for a fall guy. Just give me the rest of the time we agreed on and I'll prove to you that I've been leveling all along."

"Give me one reason why I should take your word even for what day it is."

Liddell turned to Herlehy. "There's been another homicide connected with this case. I heard this morning that they found a press agent named Les Ringer shot to death."

Herlehy scowled.

"He was found on the East Side. In an alley, according to the newscasts."

The scowl cleared. "Oh, him. A petty larceny chiseler. Far as we know he owed everybody. Probably a loan shark job."

"Inspector, Ringer was Murray Carter's finger man. He scouted the dirt for at least four articles that I know of."

The frown was back. Herlehy looked to Jacobs and back. "You think he was killed because he knew something?"

"I'm sure of it. Ringer called me yesterday, wanted to sell some information. I was to meet him at the Miss America Ballroom. He never showed up."

The assistant D.A. frowned. "How do we know you did?"

Liddell grinned. "Because I talked to two hostesses, a fat blonde and a young kid. One of them will remember me. I didn't leave there until after one."

"And then?"

Liddell shrugged. "I went to Harlem. To a joint known as Matty Lou's. If you want proof I was there, call Ed Murray at Treasury. He'll tell you that I gave him the dope on the joint that made the big raid up there early this morning possible."

Herlehy took a deep sip from his container, sat back.

"That sound like I've been crossing you?"

Jacobs ran the flats of his hands down both sides of his face. "What were you doing up there?"

"Checking out on Mike Regan's alibi. It checked." He touched the side of his jaw. "Do you think I went up against Slugger Ryan because I had nothing else to do? If I already had an idea of who the killer was, do you think I'd go to all this trouble?"

Jacobs turned to Herlehy. "Any way of checking whether these two killings were connected?"

"Ballistics." Herlehy got up, walked to the desk, picked up the phone. He gave the extension number of the Police Laboratory, told the lieutenant in charge of the physical division what he wanted, hung up the phone. "It'll take a little while. In the meantime, I'm inclined to accept Liddell's hunch."

Jacobs managed to look surprised. "But——"

"I know he works in a screwy way sometimes, but he usually levels. I'm willing to give him the benefit of the doubt." He turned to Liddell. "You say this Ringer wrote articles for Carter? On whom?"

"Celeste Pierce." The other two men exchanged glances. "Slugger Ryan, Mike Regan, Tony DeSales, Leo Dugan."

214

Marcus Jacobs leaned back, ran his fingers through his hair. "The same possibles," he groaned.

Herlehy nodded. "We might be smart if we put out an APB on all of them and dragged them in here to answer a few questions."

"The newspapers would have a picnic and all you'd get would be some fast double talk," Liddell told him.

"We're doing better with you?" the district attorney snorted.

"I'm not giving you double talk. I've eliminated a lot of names the newspapers could have a field day with. I just want the time to cut this list down and pick out your probable for you."

"You think you can do that? In twenty-four hours?" Jacobs wanted to know.

"I already think I know who killed Carter. But I still can't prove how."

"You know why he did it?"

Liddell nodded. "I'm sure of it. And the same reason holds for Les Ringer."

Jacobs squinted at him. "What do you mean you can't prove how he did it?" He turned to Herlehy. "He was shot through the head, wasn't he?"

Herlehy emptied his container, crushed it in his fist, threw it at the wastebasket. "The same thing bothers Liddell that bothers us. How can you shoot a man from only a few feet away and not leave powder burns? Also, why should a .32 bullet be so spent in that distance that it failed to come out?"

Jacobs scowled. "I hadn't heard anything about this."

Herlehy nodded. "We haven't been publicizing it. We'd rather have the answer to it before it comes up." He turned to Liddell. "That's pretty good work. For a private detective."

Liddell grinned.

"Or else you know about it because you were the one that fired the shot and knew there'd be no powder marks," he added reflectively.

"You say you know why Carter was killed," Jacobs broke in. "Why?"

"Unless I'm very much mistaken, *Bare Facts* magazine was used to bird-dog clients for Sal Minelli. Carter was killed because there was a double cross."

"You can prove this?"

"I intend to try."

Jacobs looked over to Herlehy, who shrugged. The D.A. turned back to Liddell. "Okay, I'll give you twenty-four more hours. But on this basis. If I find out you were crossing us, whether we can pin the murder on her or not, your client gets dragged into this case up to her neck."

Liddell considered, nodded. "Okay, it's a deal."

216

CHAPTER 22

After he returned
to his office, Johnny Liddell spent the next few hours
catching up on correspondence under the goading of
the orange-haired girl from the outer office. When he
finished signing the last letter he buzzed for Pinky.

She stuck her head in the door. "Yes, master?"

"You've got Celeste Pierce's number out on the
Island. Get her for me, will you?"

Pinky sighed. She checked her watch, nodded.
"It figures. It's been hours since you talked to her."
She slammed the door behind her.

After a moment, the phone buzzed. He lifted
the receiver off its hook.

"Johnny?" It was the redhead's voice. "Anything wrong?"

"No, baby. I just thought of a question I should
have asked you before now. When you left Carter's
penthouse, did you see anyone on his way up?"

The phone was silent for a moment. "Nobody. Even if I had, I probably wouldn't have noticed him. All I could think about was getting out of there."

Liddell chewed on his lower lip. "Is it possible someone might have been there while you were there? In the bedroom, say."

There was no hesitation this time. "Could be. I didn't get out of the living room." She paused for a second. "You think the killer could have been there all the time?"

"Either that or he was on his way over."

"How's it going, Johnny?"

Liddell grinned ruefully. "Just fine. I've got twenty-four hours to clean up what the D.A.'s office won't touch with a six foot pole. And if I don't they're going to make my license as extinct as a kiwi."

"It's all my fault, Johnny. I shouldn't have dragged you into it."

"Forget it. That's what I had the license for in the first place. Anyway, the last inning hasn't been played yet. I may still get a turn at bat."

"Johnny, why don't we get together for a drink? You sound like you could use some cheering up."

"I don't know, baby, I——"

"Please, Johnny. I'm going to be in town tonight anyway. I want to see you."

Liddell considered. "Okay. You know the Club Savannah?"

"I've been there."

"What time can you make it?"

There was a brief pause. "Would the midnight show be too late?"

"Just fine, baby. I'll be there."

"Okay. See you then."

Liddell dropped the receiver on its hook, leaned back, laced his hands behind his head. He didn't take them down when the door opened and Pinky entered. She walked over to the desk, picked up a cigarette.

"We bite off more than we can chew on this one, boss?" she asked.

"Could be, Pink. There's a lot of heat on this one and our friend Mark Jacobs isn't taking any more than he can help." He pursed his lips. "Can't say I blame him. There's enough pressure to push him right out of the Old Man's chair he's been coveting for so long."

Pinky lit a cigarette, walked around the desk, stuck it between Liddell's lips. "Why don't we bow out? If it's that much of a hot stove for him, it's plain dynamite for us."

"You know the old line? You're in as much hot water if you quit as you are if you go ahead? That's us." He unlaced his fingers, took the cigarette from between his lips, blew a stream of smoke at the ceiling. "The hell of it is, I think I know who did the job. But he's smart enough to know I couldn't make it stick. Without at least one witness anyway."

"Isn't there a witness around that could do it?"

Liddell considered. "Yeah, I'm sure one guy could do the job, but he'll never open his mouth." He stuck the cigarette back between his lips. "It looks like we're in a standoff, Pink. Hell, I guess I could go out and wave a gun under his nose and make him spill what he knows, but the minute I got him into the D.A.'s office he'd clam and I'd be in an even worse spot."

"Well you just can't sit here and watch your license take off. You've got to do something."

"I did, Pink. I laid it on the line how much I know and how much more I've guessed. My only hope is to sit tight and hope the witness decides to spill. If he does, I want to be handy before he can change his mind."

Pinky nodded. "You're going to stay here?"

Liddell nodded. "It's the only card I've got left to play."

"Want me to hang around?"

Liddell shook his head. "No. You go on home. I'll hold down the fort. Even if nothing happens, that way I can at least have a good night's sleep."

"Anything I can get you before I go? Want some coffee?"

Liddell shook his head. "Between you and Herlehy, my kidneys are floating in coffee."

Pinky sniffed. "They're a lot better off in that than floating in the stuff you drink." She walked hesitantly to the door. "You know, I've got a funny feeling about this. I wish you'd call Herlehy or somebody. Even Red Daniels. I've got a feeling there's going to be trouble."

"You mean something else could happen to me? My license is on the edge, I've got twenty-four hours to pull a rabbit out of the hat and everybody has clammed up on me. And you think there might be trouble?"

"Well, I hope you know what you're doing. See you in the morning." She closed the door after her.

Liddell got up, walked over to the window. The shadows were growing longer in Bryant Park. The red-dialed Enna Jettick clock on the 40th Street side of the park showed 6:45. He walked back to his chair, settled down to wait. The next time he looked at the clock it was 8:20. He had almost concluded that his pigeon was going to get away.

The phone rang at 8:27. He had difficulty recognizing the voice.

"Can I reach Liddell anyplace?"

"This is Liddell."

He could hear an indrawn breath at the other

221

end of the line. "I thought by now you'd be gone. This is Hunter. Bob Hunter. I've got to see you, Liddell."

"Where are you? I can get there——"

"No. I'll come there. Wait for me."

"Look, Hunter—" The line sounded dead. "Hunter!" Liddell clicked the cross bar. "Hunter!"

The metallic voice of the operator cut in. "Number please."

"I was connected with my party. We were cut off. Can you get them back?"

The operator's voice was polite, inflexible. "I must have the number. I'm sorry."

Liddell slammed the receiver back on its hook, cursed volubly. He got up, started to pace the office. There was no way of knowing where Hunter had called from, how long it would take him to get there —or even if he would get there.

All three questions were answered twenty minutes later with a banging on the outside office door. Liddell slipped his .45 from its holster, walked to the door. He unlocked it, pulled it open, covered the doorway with the .45.

Bob Hunter, editor of *Bare Facts*, stood in the hallway. He shied away when he saw the .45. Liddell lowered it, motioned for him to come in. He led the way to the inner office.

Hunter dropped wearily into the customer's

222

chair, watched with interest while Liddell dug into the lower drawer, came up with a bottle and two glasses. He poured a stiff jolt into each of the glasses, handed one to the editor.

"Thanks." Hunter tossed his drink off with a gulp, set the glass on the edge of the desk. "I guess you're going to think I'm crazy, but I just thought of something I think you ought to know."

"I was hoping you would." Liddell leaned back in the desk chair, waited for the other man to continue.

Hunter cleared his throat nervously. "I probably should have told you this this afternoon, but I didn't want to get mixed up in this mess any deeper than I was . . ." He paused to wet his lips with the tip of his tongue.

Johnny Liddell snagged a cigarette from the pack on his desk, nodded his encouragement.

"Well, the fact of the matter is that I think I know who killed Carter." He paused, studied Liddell's face. "I guess I knew all along but I was afraid to open my mouth."

"Minelli?"

Hunter nodded, dragged out the handkerchief, swabbed his forehead. "Yeah. Minelli."

"You willing to tell this to the police?"

"You've got to protect me."

"You'll get all the protection you need," Liddell

assured him. "Give me the picture fast. Carter softened them up and, when Minelli offered them a deal and an out, they jumped. Right?"

The editor nodded miserably. "It was going fine until Minelli insists that Celeste Pierce get the treatment. She's a real property and he wanted her in his stable. But Carter decided to use her to build up the magazine." He licked at his lips, looked at the bottle. Liddell spilled some more liquor into the glass. Hunter snagged it. "I was with Carter one day when Minelli called. They had a helluva row and Minelli told him if he double-crossed him——"

"Go on. If he double-crossed him——" Johnny Liddell was dimly aware of someone in the doorway. He looked up to see Sal Minelli standing there, his hands in his pocket. He was staring at Hunter.

"I've been looking for you, you little rat . . ."

As he started toward Hunter, the front of the editor's coat seemed to burst into flame. The roar of a .38 reverberated through the cramped space, the acrid smell of gunpowder stung their nostrils.

Minelli seemed to grow bigger as he stood on his tiptoes, then he started to fold at the knees. He tried to tug his hand out of his pocket but it had suddenly become too heavy. He went to his knees, sprawled out full length, face down on the floor. He was dead by the time Johnny Liddell reached him.

Hunter sat in the chair, gun in hand. A thin

spiral of smoke ribboned from his pocket. He stared at the dead man with wide eyes.

"Nice shooting, Hunter," Liddell grunted. "You won't need that protection any more."

The editor pulled his gun from his pocket, stared at it as though he had never seen it before. "I haven't handled one since I got out of the Army."

"How come you came here heeled tonight?" Liddell went through the dead man's pockets, dumped a .45 on the floor.

"I was afraid. The more I thought about what you said, the more I was positive that Minelli had killed Carter. I would have kept my mouth shut. I didn't want any trouble." Without being asked, he poured himself another drink. He held it to his lips, some of the bourbon ran down the side of his mouth, dripped off his chin.

"But?"

Hunter shrugged. "He must have found out that you came to see me today. He wanted to know what questions you asked, whether you mentioned him."

"And you told him."

"I told him I hadn't opened my mouth. He called me all kinds of liar and rat. He said if he found out I'd spilled anything, he'd have one of his boys give me a working over."

Liddell waited for him to continue.

"I thought of running away, but I guess I'm just tired of running. I told him if he didn't leave me alone I'd spill everything I knew to you."

"That was like spitting in a tiger's eye. What then?"

"He told me I'd never reach your place. The only place I was going was to the morgue. I told him to try and stop me." He sank his face into his hands. "I must have been crazy."

Liddell reached over, snagged the phone. "Took a lot of nerve to do what you did."

"Sooner or later even a worm gets nerve if he gets pushed hard enough." He dropped his hands, kept his eyes averted from the sprawling figure of Sal Minelli. "I had no choice, did I?"

Liddell dialed the number of headquarters. "What made you shoot?"

The editor shrugged his shoulders nervously. "I guess seeing him standing there in the doorway with his hands in his pockets. Remembering that gangsters always shot through their pockets. I—I took a chance."

Liddell spoke into the phone. "Inspector Herlehy in Homicide."

After a moment, Herlehy was on. "Herlehy."

"This is Liddell, Inspector. I've got another body for you. Sal Minelli."

"What?" Herlehy roared. "You gun-happy——"

"Not me, Inspector. Bob Hunter, Carter's editor. Minelli tried to stop Hunter from telling me what he knew of Carter's operations. He wasn't fast enough and he's cluttering up my office."

Herlehy's voice was softer. "Does Hunter know anything?"

"Plenty. His testimony will break the case."

There was a soft sigh on the other end of the phone. "Mark Jacobs will be glad to hear that."

Liddell grinned. "I'll bet he will. By the way, Inspector, I'm having a late snack with my client. I'd like you to meet her."

"Well . . ."

"Come on, Inspector. Sort of a celebration."

"Where?"

"The Club Savannah. For the midnight show. I'll be expecting you." He tossed the receiver back on its hook. "You've made the assistant district attorney very happy," he told Hunter.

"What happens to me now?"

"They'll probably hold you as a material witness. But if we can prove that Minelli killed Carter, the worst you can come out with is a medal."

CHAPTER 23

The Club Savannah
is a chromium-plated spot on the East Side. A multi-colored awning extends to the curb, a seven foot giant in an impressive getup makes a production of meeting all cabs, escorting the occupants across the sidewalk to the entrance. He made an exception in Johnny Liddell's case, just grinned a greeting.

Inside, a pert little hatcheck girl in an abbreviated costume relieved him of his hat, handed him a square cardboard ransom note for its safe return.

Angelo, a two hundred pound fashion plate in a midnight blue tuxedo, with the perennial carnation in its lapel, was guarding the entrance to the dining room beyond. When he saw Liddell, he replaced the fixed, bored smile with a genuine grin. He minced over to where Liddell stood.

"You couldn't use an assistant, could you?" he greeted the private detective.

"You mean you think there's a better racket than the one you've got? You're flipped, man, real flipped. You got it made while the rest of us have to scratch for a living."

"Maybe so, but in my racket, chicks like Celeste Pierce don't hold down a table for us. If that's scratching, Johnny, I'm starting to let my nails grow right now."

"Never mind who's holding the table. Who gets the tab?"

Angelo rolled his eyes. "For this redhead, I'd even pick up the tab myself." He shook his head. "I sure had you pegged wrong. All along I've been thinking the most exciting thing you ever did was bodyguard a couple of tin coffeepots at a wedding."

"Inspector Herlehy show up yet?"

The bantering smile faded from Angelo's face. "Inspector Herlehy? You expecting him?"

"Yeah. Matter of fact, I thought he'd get here before me."

The heavy man sighed. "No trouble, is there? I mean nothing's going to happen in here?"

"What's the matter? A citizen can't buy a public servant a drink without you expecting a catastrophe?"

"Sure. Except when the citizen is Johnny Liddell and the public servant is a homicide cop. Then

229

I get nervous." He eyed Liddell anxiously. "What gives?"

"Look. The inspector's a man. So he gets a chance to meet a dish like Pierce and he jumps at it. I'm just giving him a break."

"That'll be the day," Angelo groaned. He managed to look unhappy as he led the way back to the velvet rope that hung across the entrance to the dining room. At a snap of his finger, a captain materialized at his side.

"Table fifty-two for Mr. Liddell. Miss Celeste Pierce is expecting him." The way he said it made it sound as though St. Peter had just issued a season pass. He nodded unhappily to Liddell. "When the inspector comes, I'll send him over."

Liddell followed the wasp-waisted figure of the captain to a secluded table in the rear of the club. He earned the hatred of all the men in sight and the interested speculation of all the women by bending over, kissing the redhead lightly on the lips.

"I was afraid you mightn't be able to make it," she told him. "I heard a flash about Sal Minelli being killed."

Liddell slid into the chair opposite her. "Picked my office for it, yet. Now I'll need a new rug."

Celeste shuddered. "Don't kid about it, Johnny. That's three dead. They say it always goes in threes, don't they?"

He shrugged. "That's what they say." He turned to the waiter who hovered at his shoulder. "I'll have an Ancient Age on the rocks. How about you, baby?"

"I didn't wait for you. I have mine." She waited until the waiter had withdrawn. "Minelli— is he the one that killed Carter?"

"Carter's editor says so. Heard him threatening Carter."

Celeste took a deep swallow from her glass. "I'm glad it's all over." She reached over, covered his hand with hers. "I was so afraid you might be the third."

"Well, it's not because nobody tried." He leaned back while the waiter slid a drink in front of him. "From the minute I got on this case, a lot of people have been going out of their way to prove to me that I wasn't wanted."

The redhead pouted prettily. "I didn't."

Liddell grinned. "In some cases, gratitude can be as fatal as antagonism. But if I have to die, I can't think of a better way than gratitude."

Celeste looked around, grinned. "Lower your voice." She half veiled her eyes with heavy lashes. "I didn't know you were the kind that kisses and tells."

"Talking about telling. I didn't get your pictures back. So, I really haven't earned that gratitude yet."

The smile faded on the girl's face. "Didn't Minelli have them?"

Liddell swirled the liquor in his glass, pursed

his lips. "I got the impression that he could lay his hands on them at a moment's notice. If I could get into his files——"

"What would you do?" Inspector Herlehy stood next to the table, his hands on his hips.

Liddell looked up, startled. Then he grinned. "Nobody could ever have told me that a pair of eleven double E's could be so quiet." He shook his head. "You could give a guy a bad time sneaking up on him that way."

"You're one guy I could enjoy giving a good time." He looked from Liddell to the redhead. "You're in bad company, Miss Pierce."

She grinned at him. "Confidentially, I'm scared witless of him."

"You know Celeste Pierce, Inspector? This is Inspector Herlehy, baby."

"I do now." The inspector smothered her little hand in his big paw. "And I can understand some of your enthusiasm on this case."

A waiter sidled up, pulled out a chair, waited until Herlehy had settled himself in it.

"Off duty, Inspector?" Liddell wanted to know.

Herlehy nodded, turned to the waiter. "Chivas on the rocks." The waiter nodded, hustled toward the service bar.

"We were just talking about Minelli, Inspector. I guess Hunter gave you a statement?"

Herlehy nodded. "Sounds like you were pretty close to being right. Carter and Minelli evidently were working together to pressure top stars like Miss Pierce into Minelli's agency. They had a falling out—" he shrugged. "I don't imagine we'll declare a week of civic mourning in either case." He waited while the waiter served him. "I had a talk with Mark Jacobs. I don't think you have to worry very much about the renewal of your ticket. He said to give you his regards."

Liddell took a deep swallow from his glass. "He's satisfied the case is all wrapped up?"

Herlehy considered. "There are a few odds and ends we'd like to tie up." He shrugged. "But you won't have to worry about that. It's mostly routine."

Liddell made concentric circles on the table with the wet bottom of his glass. "There are a couple of odds and ends that I'd like to tie up myself."

Herlehy frowned. "Such as?"

"No powder burns on Carter's head, yet the shot was fired almost at contact. Who has the material and pictures belonging to my client. Part of our deal was that we get them back."

Herlehy nodded. "When they show up, you get them back. Right now our boys are up to their hips in Minelli's files. If they're there, you'll get them."

Celeste chewed on her lower lip. "Inspector, about those pictures and that story——"

The white-haired man cut her off with an up-raised palm. "Don't worry about it, Miss Pierce. We'll get them back for you. All of us have pictures and things in our background we're not too happy with. In my case, there's a passport picture making the rounds . . ."

The redhead laughed, reached over and squeezed his hand. "Thanks, Inspector. One of the few nice things that's come out of this mess is to find out that there are still men like you and Johnny around. A long time ago, I kind of lost track of them."

The inspector managed to look embarrassed. He took a swallow from his glass, turned to Liddell. "You were right on another one, Johnny. The slug they took out of Les Ringer matched the one we got out of Carter. Same gun."

Liddell nodded. "It figured. Ringer must have started wondering why certain articles he wrote appeared while others didn't. A guy like that with his ear to the ground would hear about Minelli's new clients. Sooner or later he was bound to put two and two together. And when he did, he had to die."

The redhead bit her lip, shook her head. "It's hard to believe what some men will do for money."

"Inspector, as I just told you, the material on Miss Pierce didn't show up, but I did manage to get my hands on the stuff Carter had on Slugger Ryan, Tony DeSales, Leo Dugan and Mike Regan."

"That's even better news than I hoped for. When can I get it?"

"I'd like a favor before I turn it back."

Herlehy squinted at him, a worried frown between his eyes. "A gimmick, Johnny? We had a deal. We gave you seventy-two hours, you were to turn over the material to us."

"I intend to. I just want to return it personally."

The inspector studied his face, found no explanation. "Why?"

Liddell shrugged. "Some of these characters gave me a bad time. Maybe I want to grandstand a bit."

Herlehy couldn't rid himself of the worried expression. "I get nervous when you pull one like this out of the hat. Where did you get the material?"

Liddell grinned at him. "That's not part of the deal. My part was to finger the possibles, or even to hand you the killer. I was also to hand over all the material I laid my hands on. That's what I propose to do."

Herlehy chewed on his lip thoughtfully. "You mean you want to drop in on each of these characters and hand them this material?"

"No. I'd rather do it right in front of your eyes. Then you'll know it's been done."

The redhead sat sipping her drink, watching the bargaining going on, wondering along with the inspector about Liddell's reason.

"I'll admit I'd feel better if I saw the stuff given back to these people," Herlehy conceded. "How did you figure to do it?"

"Have Jacobs call an informal meeting. Invite these people in a way they couldn't turn down. Inform them that if they'll show at his office at such and such an hour property belonging to them found in Murray Carter's possession would be returned."

"I might buy that. But I'd have to check with Jacobs."

Liddell nodded. "I'd want you to." He pointed to the lobby. "The phones are out there."

Herlehy got up, stared bleakly down at Liddell. "I might have known if you invited me for a drink there'd be a headache attached. I have your word there are no fishhooks in this one?"

"Have I ever crossed you?"

"I'm willing to let bygones be bygones. I'm only worried about are you trying to cross me on this one?"

"How can I? The people themselves will be there. They can take a look at their folders and see whether or not they're getting the real stuff."

Herlehy considered it. "It sounds so damn on the level I'm sure it's gimmicked someplace." He

236

turned to Celeste. "He's the only guy I've ever known who could turn a Christmas present into a booby trap."

Celeste grinned sympathetically. "I don't know if it's much consolation to you, Inspector, but he's never broken his word to me."

"Tell you the truth, he's never broken his word to me, either. But he's sure bent hell out of it a couple of times. Well, I guess all I've got to lose is my pension." He turned, headed for the lobby.

When he was out of earshot, the girl leaned over. "Johnny, you're not going to do anything to embarrass that wonderful old man, are you?"

Liddell shook his head. "No, baby. All I'm interested in doing is to mark this case closed. Herlehy won't be too sorry to see that either. And there's no other way I know of doing it."

He waved down a waiter for a refill all around. The drinks were just being served to the table when Herlehy lumbered back.

"Mark's a little worried. Like me." He dropped into his chair. "On my say-so, he'll play along. No publicity on this?"

Liddell nodded. "No publicity."

"Okay, we're setting up the date at Mark's office tomorrow morning at eleven. Okay with you?"

"Fine. Do you think you can turn up Slugger Ryan by then?"

"Slugger turned himself in on advice of counsel shortly after word of Minelli's death got out. Wanted to know if we were looking for him," he snorted.

"I think it might be an idea if Bob Hunter were there, too," Liddell suggested. "He'll probably know more about the material than any of us."

"No problem. Mark has him under protective custody until he can get a Grand Jury to cross it off as justifiable homicide."

"Then we'll have DeSales, Dugan, Ryan, Mike Regan and Hunter. Right?"

Herlehy nodded. "And you." He turned to Celeste. "Would you like to sit in?"

She declined with a grin. "I think I've had this case. If it's all right with you, I'll pass this one up."

"Of course."

Liddell settled back. "So, I'll see you tomorrow morning at eleven in Jacobs' office. Now what do you say we all relax and enjoy the show. No more shop talk?"

"Suits me," the inspector nodded. But when he raised his glass to his lips, his eyes were worried as they studied Liddell over the rim.

CHAPTER 24

When Johnny Liddell walked into the antechamber adjoining Mark Jacobs's office the next morning, he carried a brief case under his arm. Tony DeSales was sprawled in a chair in the corner, his legs extended at full length in front of him. He was absorbed in a study of his nails in his lap, paid no attention to the girl who sat at his side. She flashed Liddell a warm smile as he came in.

Slugger Ryan grinned crookedly at the private detective. "Hiya, champ? How's the glass jaw?" He guffawed, looked to Leo Dugan for appreciation, didn't get it. The manager contented himself instead with a scowl in Liddell's direction.

A man Liddell had never seen before got up from a chair, walked over to him with extended hand. "Liddell?"

"Yeah." He liked the firm grip of the other man.

"Matty Regis of Magna Pictures. I'm standing in for Mike Regan."

"Always glad to meet a client," Liddell grinned. "How is Regan?"

Regis pursed his lips, shook his head. "He's in real bad shape. We're just hoping we can get him on his feet for the opening tomorrow night."

"That bad, eh?"

"Yeah. He had a real skinful this time. He's a plenty foolish character. He's got a lot to lose."

In the corner, Tony DeSales squirmed uncomfortably. "How long's this going to take? I got a two o'clock show to do."

"It won't take long," Betty Marks told him. "Mr. Jacobs said it was just a formality." She dug into her bag, came up with a cigarette, held it between her fingers, looked toward Liddell.

"Pardon me, Regis." Liddell walked over to the girl, struck a match. "Hello, Betty. I see you've got your charge on a leash."

The crooner rolled his eyes up insolently, curled his lip in a sneer. "That's what I don't like about a D.A.'s office. You run into all kinds of characters."

"You ought to know, Junior," Liddell grinned. He turned to the girl. "I figured with Minelli out of the picture, you'd be turned out to pasture."

The girl smiled, shook her head. "Mr. Minelli

had a number of associates." She accented the word slightly. "They asked me to stay."

"And Junior?"

DeSales was elaborately ignoring Liddell, had returned to an examination of his fingernails in his lap.

"The new management had a talk with Tony this morning. He promised to be good," the girl smiled. "No problems."

The door to Jacobs's office opened, Herlehy stood in the doorway. He looked around, satisfied himself that everyone was there. "Okay, folks. Will you come in now?"

They filed into the room. Matty Regis stopped long enough to explain to Herlehy that he was representing Regan. Then everyone found seats on the folding chairs arranged in front of Mark Jacobs's desk.

Bob Hunter was already in the room, flashed a weak smile to Liddell as he came in. Liddell walked up to the desk, deposited the brief case on it.

Jacobs waited until everyone was seated. "Thank you all for coming. We won't take up much of your time."

"What's it all about?" Leo Dugan growled truculently.

The assistant D.A. managed a smile. "We have come into possession of certain material that belongs to you gentlemen. My office has arranged that it will be returned to you." He unstrapped the brief case, brought out a sheaf of page proofs and some glossy photographs. The photos were separated into groups, each stapled.

"These articles were in the possession of Murray Carter and were to be used in his magazine." He coughed apologetically. "They came into our possession and our best guess is that the proper owner is the person concerned. How they came into our possession, I am not at liberty to say."

"We don't care how you got them," Dugan grunted. "Let's have the stuff and call it a day. As far as I'm concerned, Minelli should have gotten a medal for knocking that rat off and——"

"Minelli didn't kill Carter, you know," Liddell broke in.

Dugan broke off in the middle of the sentence, his mouth open. He swung on Jacobs. "What is this?"

The assistant D.A. waved him to silence. "What did you say, Liddell?"

"Minelli didn't kill Carter. Sure, he had a reason to. But almost everybody in this room did, too. Slugger Ryan, for instance. He threatened to kill him on sight."

Slugger let out a roar, tried to jump to his feet, let Dugan restrain him. The manager's face was red

242

with anger. "If this was just a gimmick to get the Slugger to turn himself in, it's going to be the most expensive gimmick you ever used," he roared at Jacobs. "You couldn't even get yourself elected dog-catcher after this." He turned to the Slugger. "Come on. We're getting out of here." They started for the door.

"Sit down, Dugan," Herlehy roared at him. "I'll tell you when to go." He swung on Liddell. "As for you, Liddell, you've crossed me for the last time. You're done in this town."

Liddell reached into his pocket. "Let me fill you in. Then if you want my ticket, there it is." He tossed his credentials onto the D.A.'s desk. Jacobs opened his top drawer, swept them in.

"Minelli couldn't have killed Carter. If Carter was double-crossing him, do you think Carter would let a tough character like Minelli get in back of him?" He shook his head. "Carter wasn't killed by a guy he was that much afraid of. Besides, Inspector, did you ever know a guy who never carried anything lighter than a .45 suddenly going in for a .32?"

Herlehy looked thoughtful. "Why didn't you tell us this before?"

"Because I wasn't sure until now."

"You can't pin this rap on my boy, shamus," Dugan waved a finger at him. "You try and——"

Liddell looked over to where Ryan was breathing heavily through his nose. "I'm not trying to. I just said he had as good a reason as Minelli." He looked to Herlehy. "Ryan didn't kill him. Not that he wouldn't have if he had caught up with him. But a goon like Ryan would have done it with his bare fists. Not a gun."

DeSales jumped to his feet. He was aware of the D.A.'s eyes on him. "Oh, no you don't. You don't buy yourself a fancy rep by pinning it on me. I got some friends too who can——"

"Sit down, Junior. Nobody in their right mind would give you credit for enough guts. Minelli might have done the job for you, but you wouldn't have the nerve to do it yourself, toad sticker or no toad sticker."

Hunter sat dazed in his chair. "But yesterday you were so sure it was Minelli. You said that——"

"You knew he didn't do it all the time, Hunter. You had to know because you killed Carter."

There was a stunned silence. Hunter jumped to his feet. "That's crazy." His eyes sought the D.A. beseechingly. "That's the craziest thing I ever heard."

Liddell turned to Herlehy. "You remember one of the things that puzzled us both was how he could be shot at such close range with no powder burns?" He picked the brief case up from the desk, stuck his hand into it. From one of its folds, his index finger emerged. "When the tech men examine this, they'll find plenty of powder burns on the inside."

Herlehy strode over to where he stood, examined the brief case. "Where did you get this?"

"While you held Hunter in protective custody, I had a good chance to examine his office and hotel room. I found that in his closet."

The editor stared at the brief case with stricken eyes. "That's illegal."

"So is murder."

Mark Jacobs looked worried. "You mean he had the gun in there and shot Carter through it?"

Liddell nodded. "Eliminated powder burns and explains why the bullet was so spent in such a short distance."

"You were looking for something like this?" Herlehy asked.

Liddell nodded. "I tried to figure who Carter would let stand behind him with something that would muffle the powder burns. The most likely guy to be looking over a publisher's shoulder would be an editor while they were planning a layout. It would be logical for the editor to have an envelope or a brief case to carry the proofs back and forth. While Carter was poring over a proposed layout, Hunter stuck his hand into the brief case and shot him."

"But why?" Jacobs demanded. "Why Hunter?"

"Because Hunter was on the spot. He was about to get caught in a squeeze between Minelli and Carter and either way he was cooked."

"Stop talking all around it and give us what you know," Herlehy growled.

"Okay. It wasn't Carter that was providing Minelli with this background information on possible new clients, it was Hunter."

The editor sank back, seemed to have shrunk in his chair.

"He kept his eye peeled for possibles in the future inventory, managed to get a copy of the article and send it over to Minelli. Then Minelli would send it along to the subject and suggest that if he or she were a Minelli client, it would never run. Right, DeSales?"

The crooner bobbed his head sulkily.

"They never gave me a chance to get mine back before they used it," Slugger Ryan grunted.

"You already had a manager," Liddell pointed out, "a manager who could make you a worthless property if you ever left him. The only material Minelli bought from Hunter was on people who could switch to his agency without any loss of value."

"Then why should Hunter kill Carter?" Jacobs wanted to know.

"Because there was a slip-up. Hunter saw the advance proofs of the article on my client, sent them to Minelli and collected for them. The article wasn't scheduled to run for several months, so Minelli would have plenty of time to make a deal. But Carter kicked over the applecart by moving the article up to the next issue. Right, Hunter?"

Hunter licked his lips. "It's your crystal ball."

"The first Hunter knew about the article breaking in the next issue was when Carter told him to come to the penthouse that night. He probably told him of the plan to use the cackle bladder on my client and build it up as an attempt on his life. He figured to sell a million extra copies." He paused, looked around.

Herlehy nodded for him to continue.

"My guess is that you tried to persuade him to postpone the article, probably were showing him some other layouts. You knew that if Minelli got the idea you were crossing him, he might send some of his associates around to straighten you out. Or, he might drop a word to Carter and that might be even worse. You decided to kill Carter."

Hunter looked up. He dug a handkerchief out of his pocket, swabbed at his face. He looked around for sympathy, found none.

"Okay, so I killed him. Why shouldn't I pick up a couple of bucks from Minelli? Carter wasn't paying me enough to stay alive on." He fluttered his hands in a hopeless gesture. "But if he ever found out I was selling the stuff to Minelli, he would have had me put away. You think he didn't have something on me like on everyone else?"

"How long have you known this?" Herlehy snapped at Liddell.

Liddell shrugged. "I've only been able to prove it since I found the brief case. I figured it had to be him, but knowing and proving are two different things." He turned to the editor. "My guess was that the killer was in the bedroom all the time Carter was giving my client the cackle bladder treatment."

"I still don't see why that singled him out."

"The next morning Hunter showed me a release about the shooting. He said he was supposed to pass it out that day." Liddell shook his head. "Carter wouldn't work it that way. He'd have him there to pass the story out to the press while Carter was being carried out on a stretcher."

The D.A. nodded, squinted at Hunter. "You ready to make a statement?"

"I guess I might as well," the editor shrugged.

"On Les Ringer, as well?"

Hunter nodded.

"Why did you kill him?" Herlehy wanted to know.

"You know the old story about getting olives out of a bottle? After the first one they come easy. It's the same way with killing. Ringer had put two

248

and two together. He knew Carter wasn't selling out to Minelli and he wasn't. That left me. He gave me a chance to buy him off before he sold what he knew to Liddell."

"And you paid him off in lead."

Hunter shrugged. "They can only hang me once."

"But Minelli," Herlehy growled. "Minelli was no amateur. How come he let a character like you fog him?"

"Minelli was only half smart. He didn't tumble that I'd killed Carter until Liddell spelled it out for him. I called him and told him I was going to spill everything I knew to Liddell." He swabbed at his moist face. "He tried to talk me out of it, said if I tried to reach Liddell the only place I'd reach would be the morgue."

"Then you were ready for him when he showed up?"

Hunter nodded. "He was a sitting duck."

"I think we'd better get that over his autograph," Jacobs told the inspector. He jabbed at a button. When the uniformed man stuck his head in, Jacobs pointed to the editor. "Get a couple of stenographers on him. He's got a real interesting story to tell."

Nobody said a word as Hunter was led from the room.

"Well, let's wrap this up," Jacobs grunted. He wiped his upper lip with the side of his hand. He picked up a set of proofs, glanced at it. "This belongs to you, Ryan." He handed it to the ex-champ.

"Can I ask the Slugger a question?" Liddell asked in a deceptively mild voice. He turned to Ryan. "Have you stopped beating your mother?"

Ryan growled deep in his chest, started for the private detective. This time Liddell was waiting for him. He sidestepped the lunge, chopped at Ryan's thick neck with the side of his hand. Slugger Ryan hit the floor face first.

"Nice. Very nice," Betty Marks approved.

Liddell looked at Dugan, who was staring with open mouth at his fallen fighter. "That proves that article about him throwing that last fight was a phony. With a glass jaw like that even Baby Rose Marie could have taken him."

"I'll be damned." Dugan finally found his voice. He walked over to Ryan, turned him over on his back with the toe of his shoe. He looked up at Liddell, seemed to be seeing him for the first time. "Too bad you're not five years younger. We could make a lot of money together."

Herlehy walked over, caught Liddell by the arm. "What are you trying to do? Turn this office into a saloon?"

"Look, Inspector. My fee was to get back the

stuff they had on my client. Everybody else got theirs back free. Don't you think I deserve a little tip?"

Jacobs looked from Liddell to the inspector and back. "I think we have something that belongs to Liddell, don't we, Inspector?"

Herlehy glared at Liddell. "You got back the stuff on your client?"

Liddell nodded. "It was in the brief case Hunter had with him the night Carter was killed."

Herlehy started to say something, contented himself with running his fingers through his hair. "Give him what belongs to him, Mark, and get him the hell out of here."

Jacobs grinned at Liddell. He opened the top drawer of his desk, took out Liddell's credentials, tossed them to him. "Don't pay any attention to the inspector, Liddell. He's only saying that because he means it."

www.ingramcontent.com/pod-product-compliance
Lightning Source LLC
Chambersburg PA
CBHW020751250626
47155CB00003B/1018